‘Don’t look at me like that!’ he finally groaned harshly.

She breathed shallowly, her tongue moving to moisten suddenly dry lips. ‘Like what?’ Was that husky rasp really her voice? It had sounded completely unlike her usual confident tones, like the voice of a stranger.

Max continued to look down at her frowningly for several long, searching seconds, before flinging himself back on the pillow to stare up at the ceiling. ‘As if I’m some sort of monster you need protecting from!’ he rasped coldly.

Had she really looked at him in that way? If she had, then it was totally unfair—because the only person she needed protecting from was herself!

The Calendar Brides

They've got a date—at the altar!

International bestselling author **Carole Mortimer** has written more than 115 books, and now Modern Romance™ is proud to present her sensational new *Calendar Brides* trilogy.

Meet the Calendar sisters:
January—is she too proud to become a wife?
March—can any man tame this free spirit?
May—will she meet her match?

These women are beautiful, proud and spirited—and now they have three rich, powerful and incredibly sexy tycoons ready to claim them as their brides!

Available January, March and May 2004

HIS CINDERELLA MISTRESS

BY

CAROLE MORTIMER

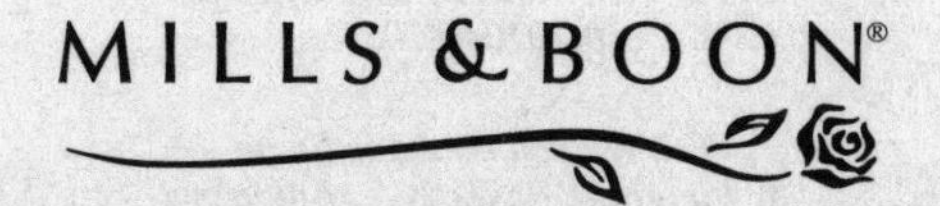

All the characters in this book have no existence outside the imagination of the author, and have no relation whatsoever to anyone bearing the same name or names. They are not even distantly inspired by any individual known or unknown to the author, and all the incidents are pure invention.

First published in Great Britain 2003
Harlequin Mills & Boon Limited,
Eton House, 18-24 Paradise Road, Richmond, Surrey TW9 1SR

ISBN 0 263 83706 8

Set in Times Roman 10½ on 12 pt.
01-0104-47055

Printed and bound in Spain
by Litografia Rosés, S.A., Barcelona

CHAPTER ONE

'WOULD you allow me to buy you a drink?'

Sitting at the bar, sipping a glass of sparkling water, taking a well-earned rest after an hour of singing, January turned to politely refuse the offer. Only to have that refusal stick in her throat as she saw who it was doing the offering.

It was him!

The man who had been seated at the back of this hotel bar for the last hour as she sat at the piano and sang. The man who had stared at her for all of that time with an intensity that had made it impossible for her not to have noticed him in return.

She should refuse his offer, had learnt to keep a certain polite distance between herself and the guests who stayed at this prestigious hotel, transient people for the most part, here for a few days, never to be seen again.

Remember what happened on the farm last year, her sister May would have told her. January did remember—only too well!

Remember what you told me—afterwards, her sister March would have said; taking people at face value only brings trouble!

'That would be lovely, thank you,' January accepted huskily.

The man gave an inclination of his dark head, ordering a bottle of champagne from John, the barman, before standing back to allow her to precede him to his table in the corner of the luxuriously comfortable room, made even more so at the moment because, although Christmas had come and gone, the decorations wouldn't be taken down for several more days yet.

January was aware of several curious glances coming their way as they walked by the crowded tables, could see their reflection in one of the mirrors along the walls. She, tall and willowy in the long black spangly dress she wore to perform in, her dark hair cascading down over her shoulders, eyes a mysterious dark smoky grey, fringed by sooty black lashes. The man walking so confidently behind her, the epitome of tall, dark and handsome in the black dinner suit and snowy white shirt he wore, his eyes a deep, unfathomable cobalt-blue.

It was those eyes, so intense and compelling, that had drawn her attention to him an hour ago, shortly after she began her first session of the evening. Those same eyes that even now, she could see in the mirror, were watching the gentle sway of her hips as she walked.

He stood to one side as January sank gracefully into one of the four armchairs placed around the low table, waiting until she was seated before lowering his considerable height into the chair opposite hers, that intense gaze having remained on her for the whole of that time.

'Champagne?' January prompted throatily a few minutes later—when it became apparent he wasn't going to make any effort to begin a conversation, seeming quite happy to just stare at her.

He gave a slight inclination of his head. 'It is New Year's Eve, after all,' he came back softly.

End of conversation, January realized a few seconds later when he added nothing further to that brief comment, beginning to wish she had listened to those little voices of her sisters' earlier inside her head.

'So it is,' she answered dismissively, smiling up at John as he arrived with two glasses and the ice-bucket containing the bottle of champagne, deftly opening it before her anonymous companion nodded his thanks—and his obvious dismissal.

John turned to leave, but not before he had given January a speculative raise of his eyebrows.

Well aware that she always kept herself slightly aloof from the guests staying at the hotel, John was obviously curious as to why this man should be so different. Join the club!

'January.' She turned back to the man determinedly.

He gave the semblance of a smile as he leant forward to pour the two glasses of champagne himself, competently, assuredly, not a single drop of the bubbly liquid reaching the top of the glass to spill over. 'That's what usually follows December,' he drawled dismissively.

'No, you misunderstood me.' She shook her head, smiling. 'My name is January.'

'Ah.' The smile deepened, showing even white teeth against his tanned skin. 'Max,' he supplied as economically.

Not exactly a scintillating conversationalist, she decided, studying him over the rim of her champagne glass. The strong, silent type, maybe, the sort of man who only spoke when he had something significant to say.

'Short for Maximillian?' she asked lightly.

His smile faded, leaving his face looking slightly grim. 'Short for Maxim. My mother was a great reader, I believe,' he added scornfully.

Her eyes widened at his tone. 'Don't you know?'

His gaze narrowed. 'No.'

Obviously not a subject to be pursued!

'And are you in the area on business, Max?' she prompted curiously; after all, it was New Year's Eve, a time when most people would be with family or friends.

'Something like that.' He nodded tersely. 'Do you work at the hotel every night, or just New Year's Eve?'

She found herself frowning slightly, unsure whether he had meant the question to sound insulting—as it did!—or whether it was just his usual abruptness of manner.

She shrugged, deciding to give him the benefit of the doubt—for the moment. 'I work here most Thursday, Friday and Saturday evenings,' she added the last pointedly.

'And as this is a Friday—'

'Yes,' she confirmed huskily. 'Look, I'm afraid I have to go back on in a few minutes,' she added with a certain amount of relief; this man was more than a little hard going!

He nodded. 'I'll wait for you at the end of the evening.' He had so far made no effort to drink any of his own champagne, merely continued to look at January with that almost blinkless stare.

Which was just as unnerving close up as it had been from the distance for the last hour while she sang!

She had accepted his invitation on impulse—curiosity?—and now she was regretting it. Okay, so his brooding stillness made Heathcliff and Mr Rochester, two of her favourite romantic heroes, seem almost chatty by comparison, but it was also extremely uncomfortable to be stared at in this single-minded fashion.

She gave a brief shake of her head. 'I don't think so, thank you.' She smiled to take some of the bluntness out of her own words; after all, he was a guest at the hotel, and she just another person employed here. 'Usually I finish about one-thirty, two o'clock, depending on how busy we are, but as tonight is New Year's Eve I'm here until three o'clock.'

And by the time she had driven home it would be almost four o'clock, by which time she would be physically shattered but mentally unable to relax, which meant she would stay up until her sisters woke shortly before six. Not an ideal arrangement by any means, but she knew she was lucky to have found this job so close to home at all, so beggars couldn't be choosers.

'I'll still wait,' Max answered her evenly.

A perplexed frown furrowed her brow; this was exactly the reason she had always kept a polite, if friendly, distance between herself and the male guests staying at the hotel. What had prompted her to make an exception in this man's case…?

She felt a shiver run down the length of her spine—of pleasure or apprehension?—as that deep blue gaze moved slowly down over the bareness of her shoulders in the strapless dress, the gentle swell of her breasts, the slenderness of her waist. Almost as if those long, artistically elegant hands had actually touched and caressed her!

'I'll wait,' he repeated softly. 'After all, what's a few more hours…?' he added enigmatically.

Very reassuring—she didn't think! In fact, there was a decidedly unsettled feeling in the pit of her stomach, accompanied by mental flashes of those recent newspaper articles about lone women being attacked in this area late at night.

Not that this obviously wealthy and assured man gave the impression of being in the category of the Night Striker—as the more lurid tabloids had dubbed him—but then, what did an attacker actually look like? The other man probably appeared perfectly normal during the day, too—it was only at night that he turned into a monster! She didn't—

'Tell me, January—' Max sat forward intently now, that dark blue gaze once again unfathomable as he looked at her face '—do you believe in love at first sight?'

The hand holding her champagne glass shook slightly at the unexpectedness of his question, her movements carefully deliberate as she placed the glass down on the table in front of her.

What had happened to the social pleasantries? The 'hello, how are you?' The 'do you have any family?' The 'when you aren't singing what do you like to do?' How did you go straight from 'how often do you work at the hotel?' to 'do you believe in love at first sight?' The obvious answer to that was—you didn't!

January's features softened into gentle mockery. 'In a word—no,' she dismissed derisively. 'Lust at first sight—maybe. But love? Impossible, don't you think?' she scorned softly.

He didn't so much as blink at her mocking reply. 'I was asking you,' he reminded softly.

'And I said no.' She was beginning to feel slightly rattled by this man's sheer force of will. 'How can you possibly fall in love with someone without even knowing them? What happens when you discover all those annoying little habits that weren't apparent at first sight?' she attempted to lighten the conversation. 'Like not squeezing the toothpaste from the bottom of the tube? Like reading the newspaper first and leaving it in a mess? Like walking around barefoot whenever possible? Like—'

'I get the picture, January,' he cut in dryly, something like warmth lightening the intense blue of his eyes. 'Are you telling me that you do all those things?'

Was she? Well…yes. And the toothpaste thing annoyed March to the point of screaming. And May was always complaining about what a mess she made when she read the newspaper. As for walking about barefoot—that was something she had done since she was a very small child; it was also something that was totally impractical when you lived in a working farmhouse. Once she had stepped on a plank of wood and ended up with a nail stuck in her foot, followed by a trip to the hospital for a tetanus injection, and another time she had stepped on a hot coal that had fallen out of the fire, again followed by a trip to the local hospital.

'I've been assured that love is supposed to nullify things like that,' Max continued dryly at her lack of reply. 'After all, no one is one-hundred-per-cent perfect.'

She had a feeling that this man might be, had a definite intuition that he would never squeeze the toothpaste tube in the middle, or leave the newspaper in a mess, and as for walking about barefoot—! No, this man gave the impression that everything he did was deliberate, carefully thought through, without fault. But perhaps that was a fault in itself…?

Although why she was even giving his question any serious thought she had no idea; it was simply ridiculous to suggest you could fall in love with the way someone looked!

'It may do, Max—but it doesn't stop hundreds of couples arriving in the divorce courts every year claiming incompatibility because of "unreasonable behaviour" by one or other partner,' she derided.

He smiled, his gaze definitely warmer now. 'I don't think they're referring to how you do or do not squeeze a tube of toothpaste,' he drawled.

'Probably not.' She shrugged. 'But I believe I've adequately answered your initial question.' Although why he had asked it at all was beyond her.

Next time she had an impulse like this, she would ignore it—no matter how handsomely intriguing the man was!

'More than adequately,' he confirmed derisively. 'And I have to say, January, it's very unusual to meet a woman with such an honest view to what everyone else chooses to romantically call love.'

January eyed him warily; she didn't think she had actually said that was the way she felt towards falling in love! 'It is?'

'It is,' he confirmed softly. 'But—'

'January, I'm really sorry to interrupt.' John, the barman, appeared beside their table.

'Not at all.' She turned to him with a certain amount of relief. 'Is it time for me to go back on?' she asked hopefully; she really had had enough of this conversation. And Max…

John grimaced. 'I just thought I should let you know Meridew is on the prowl again,' he warned, referring to the over-efficient manager of the hotel who had just strolled into the lounge bar, his gaze sweeping critically over the room.

Strictly speaking January wasn't exactly a member of the hotel staff, but that didn't stop Peter Meridew, the hotel manager, having his say if he was displeased about something. January had never tested him before on having a drink with one of the hotel guests, but perhaps that came under the heading of 'displeasing' him? Whatever, January needed this job too much to risk losing it over a man she would never see again after this evening.

'Thanks, John.' She smiled up at him before turning back to Max. 'I really do have to go.' She managed to keep her voice evenly unemotional as she prepared to leave.

Max's gaze narrowed. 'Would you like me to have a word with him?'

'Who—? Certainly not,' she protested frowningly as she saw he was now looking at the hotel manager. Although no doubt a word in Peter's ear from this assuredly arrogant man would ensure that no word was ever mentioned to her about sitting down to have a drink with him! 'It's time for me to go back on, anyway,' she dismissed lightly.

Max nodded. 'I'll be waiting here when you've finished.'

January opened her mouth to protest for a third time, and then thought better of it; what was the point? Besides, she was quite capable of slipping quietly away at the end of the evening without this man even being aware she had done so…

She stood up. 'Thank you for the champagne.'

'You're welcome.' He nodded.

January was aware of him once again watching her as she crossed the room to the piano, knowing he would see a tall, beautiful brunette in a sexy black dress. But that was all he would see—because he knew nothing else about her but her name.

Max should see her at half-past six tomorrow morning, up to her wellington-booted ankles in mud, as she trekked through the farmyard to the cow shed for early milking!

What on earth did he think he was doing? Max remonstrated with himself with an inward groan.

Was he trying to frighten the woman away before he even had chance to get to know her? Or—more importantly!—her him? If he was, he was certainly succeeding!

He hadn't wanted to come on this particular business trip at all, would have been quite happy to stay where he was until after the New Year, had been enjoying the mild, if unsuccessful, flirtation with the actress April Robine, a woman at least ten years older than his own thirty-seven, but looking at least twenty years younger than her actual age.

But it had been pointed out to him quite strongly, by his friend and employer, that these negotiations needed to be settled as quickly as possible, and it was his job, after all. Never mind the fact that Jude was as interested in April Robine as he was—and probably with more success, if he knew Jude. Which he did. Only too well.

How could Max possibly have known that a chance drink in the piano-bar of the hotel he was staying in would completely erase April, and every other woman he had ever known, from his mind, would result in his seeing the one woman he knew he had to have for his own?

Well…for a time, anyway; if he was honest with

himself there wasn't a woman in the world he wanted permanently in his life. No matter how beautiful. And January was incredibly beautiful.

She was perfect, from the top of her ebony head to the soles of her delicate feet in those ridiculously strappy sandals she was wearing.

So perfect that he hadn't been able to take his eyes off her the whole time he had been sitting here. So perfect that he had been uncharacteristically tongue-tied in her company. Except when he had asked her if she believed in love at first sight…

And been totally stunned—if pleasantly surprised!—by the honesty of the answer she had given him.

But, then, he had been stunned in one way or another since the moment he'd first looked at her, felt as if he had been punched in the stomach then, felt completely poleaxed now that he had actually spoken to her, her voice huskily sexy, her face even more beautiful close to, and as for her body…!

Perhaps he had better not dwell on the wonder of her willowy body just now; after all, it wasn't even midnight yet, which meant there were at least another three hours or so before he could take her out of here.

They were the longest three hours of his life, Max decided as he waited impatiently for January to play her final song. He hadn't even been able to get close to her when the clocks had struck midnight, had been forced to watch from afar as she'd made the countdown and had then been surrounded by well-wishers. Most of them male, he had noted with dark disapproval. All of whom he had wanted to punch on the nose as they'd claimed a New Year kiss from her.

The hotel manager had claimed her attention during her next break, the two of them talking comfortably together until it had been time for January to go back on. While Max had sat frustratedly at his table just willing her to look in his direction. Which she hadn't.

Deliberately so? After the way he had come on so strongly earlier, he wouldn't be in the least surprised!

How Jude, his longtime friend and boss, would have laughed if he could see him now! Or, more likely, having seen her, Jude would have made a play for January himself…

Now there was a thought he would rather not have had!

Ordinarily it wouldn't have bothered him if Jude was interested in the same woman he was, but he already knew January was different; it would certainly test his long-term friendship with Jude if he were to make any sort of move on her!

When at last she had finished January looked extremely tired, he noted frowningly as he stood up to join her. Not that he was in the least tired himself; jet lag had ensured that he slept this afternoon and now felt wide awake.

'Where are you going?' he prompted as she turned away without looking up.

Smoky grey eyes looked up at him guardedly beneath sooty lashes. 'Home?' she suggested ruefully.

She really did look very tired, Max noted with a frown, dark shadows beneath those incredibly beautiful grey eyes, a weariness to her shoulders too now that she was no longer on public display, the hotel guests and New Year's Eve visitors making their way noisily from the bar.

'I said I would wait for you,' he reminded huskily.

She frowned, seeming on the point of protest, one look at his obvious expression of determination making her shrug defeatedly instead. 'I just have to go and collect my coat and bag,' she told him lightly.

'I'll come with you,' Max told her firmly; having found her, he wasn't about to let her escape him now.

Those dark brows rose mockingly. 'To the women's staff room?'

He grimaced. 'I'll wait outside.'

A look of irritation flickered briefly across her creamy brow at his obvious persistence. 'Fine,' she finally acknowledged tersely. 'Give me a few minutes,' she added lightly before going into the room clearly marked 'Staff Only'.

He wasn't quite sure he could wait much longer to be alone with her. Patience had never been one of his virtues, even less so now it seemed.

But as the minutes passed with no sign of her return it appeared he didn't have much choice in the matter. Where the hell was she?

'Can I be of any assistance?' the manager—Peter Meridew?—paused to enquire politely.

Max turned to him scowlingly, the memory of how this man had monopolized January's company during her next—and only—break, still fresh in his mind. 'Is there another way out of this room?' he prompted hardly, more convinced than ever as the minutes passed that she had somehow managed to elude him.

The other man glanced at the door, his brows raised in surprise as he turned back to Max. 'Why, yes, there is,' he answered slowly, obviously perplexed by a guest's interest in what was clearly marked as a staff only room. 'It opens out into the adjacent corridor, but— Is there anything I can do to help?' the manager prompted at Max's fierce scowl.

'Not unless your name is January,' Max muttered

impatiently. 'Which it clearly isn't!' he added frustratedly.

Damn it, she had got away, he was sure of it, knew she had deliberately gone out of this staff room through another door.

Why was he so surprised? a little voice taunted inside his head; he had come onto her so strongly earlier that he must have sounded like a bored businessman just looking for a female to share his bed for the night!

And wasn't that exactly what he was?

No, it wasn't, damn it! He already knew that one night with January simply wouldn't be enough. And given a little more time in her company, he might have been able to convince her of that.

Don't be too sure of that, that little voice taunted again.

'I'm sorry?' The manager looked more confused than ever at Max's mutterings. 'Is January a friend of yours?' the other man prompted tightly.

Max drew in a deep, controlling breath, aware that January had left his table earlier as soon as she had been informed of the manager's presence in the room. After all, what was the saying, 'tomorrow is another day'…? And as, in this case, tomorrow was a Saturday, Max at least knew where she was going to be tomorrow evening…

'Not yet,' he answered the manager enigmatically. 'By the way—' he turned his full attention on the other man now, his smile at its most charming '—I would like to compliment you on the smooth and efficient running of your hotel. I travel all over the world on business, and this is definitely of a world-class standard.'

The other man visibly preened at this effusive

praise—as he was meant to do; the last thing Max wanted to do was make things difficult for January at her place of work. With any luck, Max's words of praise would override any of this man's previous curiosity as to Max's interest in January.

'It's very kind of you to say so.' The other man beamed.

'Not at all,' Max continued lightly. 'It's refreshing to stay at such an obviously well-managed hotel.' Too effusive? Not if the other man's flush of pleasure was anything to go by.

'If you require any assistance during the remainder of your stay, please don't hesitate to call on me personally,' Peter Meridew told him in parting.

Well, there was one happy man, at least, Max acknowledged ruefully as he watched the other man's retreating back.

Wishing that he could feel the same, Max sobered heavily, his earlier annoyance at what he was sure were January's evasive tactics returning with a vengeance.

But if she thought she would succeed in avoiding him for ever, she was in for a surprise.

A big surprise!

CHAPTER TWO

'MAY, what on earth is wrong with you today?' January frowned concernedly at her eldest sister, May having dropped one of the plates as the three of them stood up to clear away after eating their dinner.

May had been banging the pots and pans around serving the meal when January had come downstairs earlier, had been very quiet during dinner, only adding the odd grunt to the conversation between January and March as the three of them had eaten.

The three sisters—May, twenty-seven; March, twenty-six, and January, twenty-five—were very alike to look at, all tall and dark-haired, with a creamy magnolia skin—although that tended to colour to a healthy tan during the summer months. Only their eyes were different, May's green, March's a mixture of green and grey, and January's smoky grey.

But May, being the eldest, had always been the calm, unruffled one, able to deal with any emergency. Something she certainly didn't seem to be doing this evening!

'Still tired from doing the pantomime?' January sympathized.

Completely absorbed in the farm most of the time, May had found an outlet from that several years ago by joining the local drama group. They had put on the pantomime *Aladdin* in the small local theatre over the Christmas period, with May being given the leading role, traditionally played by a female. It had been tiring but fun, but had necessitated May being involved in evening and matinée performances over several days, as well as working on the farm.

'If only it were that...' May looked up now from picking up the pieces of broken plate. 'We had a visitor today,' she stated flatly.

January instantly stiffened, wary of whom that 'visitor' might have been; she might have escaped from the intense Max the night before, but she doubted he was a man who cared to be fobbed off by anyone. Quite how he might have found out where she lived, she had no idea, but she doubted even that was beyond him...

May's green eyes swam with unshed tears as she straightened. 'You remember that letter we had before Christmas? The one from that lawyer on behalf of some big American corporation? About buying the farm,' she prompted as both March and January looked blank.

'Of course we remember it. Damned cheek!' March scorned as she grabbed some kitchen towel to wipe up the mess from the plate that had landed on the stone floor. 'If we were interested in selling then we would have put the farm on the market.' She threw the soiled towel deftly into the bin.

'Yes,' May sighed, sitting down heavily in a kitchen chair. 'Well, the lawyer came in person to see us today. Or rather me, as I was the only one available at the time.' She grimaced.

January, as was her usual routine on the nights she was working, had been in bed most of the day, and March had been out making the most of the New Year's Day public holiday as she had a job she went to from nine till five Monday to Saturdays usually. May was the only sister who worked full-time on their small hillside farm, who also did most of the cooking and cleaning, too. It wasn't the most ideal arrangement, meant that they all effectively had two jobs, but the farm just wasn't big enough to support all three sisters without the additional financial help of January's and March's outside employment.

Their visitor obviously hadn't been the intense Max, but January wasn't sure she liked the sound of this particular visitor, either.

'I thought it was all just some sort of joke.' January frowned now as she could see just how upset her eldest sister was.

May gave a humourless laugh. 'This lawyer didn't seem to think so,' she muttered. 'In fact, he went so far as to offer an absolutely ridiculous price for the farm.' She scowled as she quoted the price.

January gasped, March swallowed hard; all of them knew that the farm wasn't worth anywhere near as much as the offer being made. Which posed the question, why was this lawyer offering so much for what was, after all, only forty acres of land, a few outbuildings, and a far from modern farmhouse?

'What's the catch?' March prompted shrewdly.

'Apart from immediate vacancy, there didn't seem to be one,' May answered slowly.

'Apart from—! But we were all born here,' January protested incredulously.

'This is our home!' March said at the same time.

May gave the semblance of a smile. 'I told him that. He didn't seem impressed.' She shrugged.

'Probably because he lives in some exclusive penthouse apartment somewhere,' March muttered disgruntledly. 'He wouldn't recognize a ''home'' if he were invited into one. You didn't invite him in, I hope?' she said sharply.

May gave a firm shake of her head. 'I was outside loading hay onto the trailer for feeding when he arrived. Once he had introduced himself, and his reason for being here, I made sure we stayed outside in the yard. His tailor-made suit certainly wasn't suitable for visiting a hillside farm in January, and he got his highly polished handmade shoes all muddy, too,' she added dryly.

January laughed at her elder sister's look of satisfaction. 'And you sent him away with a flea in his ear, I hope!'

'Mmm.' May nodded, that frown back between clear green eyes. 'But I have a distinct feeling he'll be back.'

'What's it all about, do you think?' January frowned her own concern.

'Oh, that's easy,' March answered dismissively. 'The same corporation this lawyer represents bought the Hanworth estate a couple of months ago for development of some kind. And with our farm smack in the middle of the Hanworth land...' She shrugged. 'I expect we're rather in the way.'

James Hanworth, the local equivalent of 'squire' the last fifty-five years, had died six months ago, leaving no wife or children to inherit his vast estate, just half a dozen distant relatives who had obviously decided to sell the place and divide the profits.

'Why didn't you tell us that before?' May turned to March impatiently. 'No wonder they're trying to buy us out!' she added disgustedly.

Yes, no wonder, January mentally agreed. But this farm had first belonged to her grandparents, and then her parents, and now the three sisters, and, although it was sometimes a struggle to financially survive, selling it wasn't something any of them had ever considered. It was the only home they had ever known...

She gave a glance at her wrist-watch. 'Look, I have to get ready for work now, but we'll talk about this further over breakfast in the morning, okay?'

'Okay,' May nodded ruefully.

January reached out to give her sister's arm a comforting squeeze. 'No one can make us sell if we don't want to.'

'No,' her eldest sister sighed. 'But, stuck in the middle like this, they could make life very difficult for us if they choose to.'

'Depends what sort of development they're thinking of having,' March put in thoughtfully. 'I'll check into that tomorrow and see what I can find out.'

'Don't get yourself into trouble over it,' May warned in her concerned mother-hen way. As the eldest of the three sisters, having lost their mother when they were all very young, May had taken on the role of matriarch at a very early age, and after the death of their father the previous year she now took that role doubly seriously.

'Don't worry, I won't.' March grinned dismissively, always the more reckless sister of the trio.

'I'll see you both in the morning,' January told them laughingly, well accustomed to the battle of wills that often ensued between her cautious and more impetuous sisters.

She hurried up the stairs to get herself ready for this evening, choosing another black dress this time, knee-length, with a low neckline and long black sleeves ending in a dramatic vee at her slender wrists. Her hair she pulled back with jewelled combs, leaving wispy tendrils against her creamy cheeks.

It was slightly strange to lead these double lives, dressing glamorously for her role as a singer compared to the usual thick baggy jumpers, old denims and wellington boots when she was on the farm. Somehow the two didn't seem compatible…

It was troubling about the farm, though, she considered on her drive to the hotel. As March was only too keen to point out, no one could force them to sell if they didn't want to—which they certainly didn't. But what May had said was also true: life could be made very difficult for them if some sort of development completely surrounded their land and the farm.

There were such things as right of way, and water rights, for one thing; James Hanworth had never troubled about such things, had accepted that the Calendar farm was adjacent to his, and that access and water were a necessary part of its success. Somehow January doubted the new owner—a corporation, no less—would be quite as magnanimous.

It was testament to how troubling she found the situation that she hadn't even given the man Max a second thought until she went into the almost deserted piano-bar and found him sitting there chatting to John, the barman!

For some reason she had assumed Max would only be staying at the hotel the previous night. Erroneously, as it turned out.

'Ah, January.' Max turned to look at her with mocking blue eyes as she went straight over to the piano to arrange her music for the evening. He strolled over to stand only feet away from her. 'I believe there was some sort of confusion last night as to where we were to meet each other at the end of the evening?'

He believed no such thing, knew very well that she had deliberately slipped away through another door in order to avoid meeting him.

'Was there?' January raised her head to look at him, her gaze steady—despite the fact that she felt an inner quiver of awareness at the physical impact of his attractiveness in the lounge suit and blue shirt.

He really was a very attractive man, and January would be deceiving herself if she denied responding to that attraction. It was his sheer intensity of personality that she found a little overwhelming.

'I like to think so.' He smiled, a pulse-jumping, heart-stopping smile.

As if to give lie to her wariness of his previous intensity… 'Maybe we can do better this evening?' he suggested mildly.

He really was trying to lighten up, wasn't he? January accepted with an inner amusement. But not hard enough to conceal the fact that he was still determined to spend time alone with her…

'Perhaps,' she returned noncommittally. 'If you'll excuse me? I have to start my first session,' she added to take the bluntness out of her previous statement.

'Of course,' he accepted lightly, moving back slightly to allow her to seat herself at the piano, before bending forward, his mouth only inches from her ear. 'You're looking even more beautiful this evening than you did last night,' he murmured huskily, the warmth of his breath stirring the tendrils of hair against her cheeks.

January swallowed hard, tilting her head back slightly to look up into his face. A face still only mere inches away from hers… 'Thank you,' she accepted softly.

Max straightened, that smile back on his lips as he looked down at her admiringly. 'Very graciously said,' he told her appreciatively.

January gave a mocking inclination of her head, determined not to let him see that his proximity was unnerving her. Even if it was! 'I like to think so,' she dryly returned his own comment of a few minutes ago.

He chuckled appreciatively. 'I'll have a drink waiting for you at the bar when you have your break. John tells me that you usually prefer a sparkling water.'

She gave an irritated frown at the thought of this man discussing her likes and dislikes with a third person, even someone as innocuous as John. 'The whole point of my having a break is to give me a few minutes to relax.' Something she certainly couldn't do around him!

'Then we won't talk,' he promised lightly.

No one could have accused him of being a chatterbox the previous evening! But this man didn't need to say anything to totally disrupt her equilibrium; just having him sitting there staring at her was enough to make her nervous.

'Fine,' she accepted tautly.

Max looked at her consideringly for several long seconds. 'The last time you agreed with me so readily you made an escape out the back door,' he said slowly.

January felt the guilty colour warm her cheeks; she had said and done exactly that, hadn't she…?

'Well, this time I won't,' she assured him impatiently. 'Okay?'

'Okay,' he acknowledged with a slight inclination of his head. 'By the way…' he paused before leaving

'...you have the most incredibly sexy voice, speaking or singing, that I have ever heard,' he told her softly before walking away.

Oh, very conducive to calming her already frayed nerves—she didn't think!

Better, Max, he congratulated himself as he resumed his seat on a stool at the bar. Much better. Just the right balance of humour and determination. All he had to do now was keep it up for the next few hours!

All! When January had walked into the room a short time ago wearing that figure-hugging black dress, showing a long expanse of shapely legs beneath its knee-length, he had literally stopped breathing for several seconds, the blood singing heatedly in his veins, and as for the rest of his body—! That sort of response just at the sight of a woman hadn't happened to him since he was a raw teenager!

But he had regrouped, he assured himself, had spoken to her confidently and yet not too forcefully, infusing humour into the banter they had exchanged.

And then he had told her how sexy he found the sound of her voice!

Okay, okay, so he had slipped back a little there. But it had been worth it—if only to see the warm colour that had suffused her cheeks, the sparkle in those incredibly beautiful grey eyes!

At thirty-seven, Max had known many beautiful and accomplished women, been involved with several of them, but those women had been far too worldly-wise themselves to blush at something that was said to them; it was refreshing to know that January wasn't such a sophisticate.

How old was she? he wondered. Mid-twenties, probably, he decided. Not too young that he felt guilty over this single-minded interest he had found in her, but not too old that she had forgotten how to blush at a compliment.

'Great girl, isn't she?' The barman spoke admiringly as he stood polishing glasses in preparation for the busy evening ahead, obviously having followed Max's line of vision. 'Not in the least stand-offish like some of the singers we've had in here in the past,' John added with a pointed grimace.

Max sensed that John could be a great source of information about January. If Max chose to pursue it. Which he didn't…

For some reason he felt a great need to get to know January for himself, to unpeal each protective layer, until he knew her totally. Like that parcel in the children's game where you took one wrapper off at a time as the music stopped, until at last you arrived at the treasure within.

Once again he thanked his lucky stars that his good friend Jude wasn't about to witness his interest in January; he had no doubt that the other man would have found it highly amusing to see Max floundering around in the throes of this unexpected attraction!

Amusing? He doubted Jude would be able to stop laughing for a week!

Although Max's total lack of success so far in the main reason for his being here would probably wipe that smile from the other man's face, Max conceded with a frown as he thought of his meeting earlier today. A more stubborn, unyielding—! Not that he had given up, not for a moment—it was just going to take a little longer to accomplish what he had come here to do than he had at first supposed. But now that he had met

January, that delay certainly wasn't a drawback, as far as he was concerned!

He had the distinct impression that January was going to be an even harder conquest than the business deal he had come here to complete on Jude's behalf!

The piano-bar slowly filled up as the sound of January singing drifted through to the other reception rooms, a rather noisy party of young men obviously on a stag-night part of the crowd that now stood at the bar, several of those young men obviously ogling January in her sexy black dress. Giving him the hitherto unknown feelings of jealousy at the thought of any man looking at her but him!

Which was ridiculous, considering her choice of career; the way she looked was as much a part of that career as her sexily attractive voice.

All well and good, Max, he derided his own logic—but that still didn't stop the need he felt to get up and wrap his jacket around her so that she was hidden from any other male eyes but his!

'Whisky,' he turned to order from John grimly. 'Make it a double,' he added harshly as one of the young men strolled over to chat with January as she turned the music over between songs.

John gave him a quizzical look as he set the whisky glass down in front of Max. 'January knows how to take care of herself,' he offered lightly by way of advice.

Little comfort, when Max wanted to take care of her himself. Take care of her! He wanted to pick her up in his arms, carry her up to his hotel suite and make love to her until they were both too weak to do anything else but lay satiated in each other's arms. And then he wanted to start all over again!

She was laughing up at the young man now, completely relaxed in his company. But it was too much for Max, just too much, when the young man bent his head to give January a less-than-brotherly kiss on the lips!

He wasn't even aware of crossing the room, let alone having grabbed hold of the collar of the other man's jacket as he pulled him forcibly away from January, his face only inches away from the young man's as he glared down at him.

'Max…?' January gasped softly from somewhere behind him. 'What do you think you're doing?' she snapped incredulously.

Max narrowed his gaze briefly on the younger man before he turned to look questioningly at January. 'He was bothering you—'

She was standing now, shaking her head frowningly. 'Josh is a friend, Max,' she murmured as she gently released his hand from the other man's jacket. 'He's marrying my cousin Sara next Saturday,' she added pointedly.

That may be so, Max accepted grimly, but the kiss he had given January had looked far from 'cousin-in-lawly' to him!

'You're causing a scene,' January muttered awkwardly.

Several people in the now crowded bar were watching them curiously, the group of young men who had come in with Josh amongst them. Probably getting ready to come to the aid of their friend, Max conceded self-derisively.

'Sorry,' he muttered to Josh as the younger man straightened his jacket, aware that the manager, Peter

Meridew, was also watching the exchange with a narrowed gaze.

January was right, what on earth had he thought he was doing? He might know that he was more interested in January than any other woman he had ever met, but as far as she was concerned he was merely a guest at the hotel who had bought her a drink last night!

He forced himself to relax. 'I really do apologize if I overreacted just now,' he told the other man more amiably.

'No problem,' Josh assured him dismissively. 'It's nice to know that someone is looking out for January,' he added magnanimously.

'I don't—'

'Perhaps I could buy you and your friends a drink?' Max cut in lightly on what he was sure was going to be January's assertion that she didn't need, or want, anyone looking out for her. 'I'm sure January would love to join us once she's finished this session,' he added challengingly.

January was more beautiful than ever when she was angry, Max discovered as he turned to her with raised brows, her eyes a deep sparkling grey, her cheeks flushed against magnolia skin, even her mouth appearing redder. And more kissable than ever, he realized uncomfortably.

'The wedding is next Saturday, you say?' He turned back to the younger man—as much for his own peace of mind as to break his gaze away from January's fierce glare.

'Three o'clock.' Josh grinned happily. 'You're more than welcome to accompany January, if you would care to,' he invited warmly.

'You—'

'Why don't we go back to the bar and talk about that?' Max suggested firmly at what he guessed was going to be January's heated refusal to that suggestion. 'We really shouldn't interrupt you any longer,' he told her dismissively, turning away with Josh to walk back to the bar.

But he was aware of January's glaring gaze every step of the way!

Was equally sure that her next choice of song, something about 'surviving' and being 'able to take care of herself', was in direct response to what she believed to be his heavy-handed interference a few minutes ago.

So much for his keeping the evening light and amusing, he acknowledged self-derisively. He very much doubted that she would consider his almost punching her cousin-in-law-to-be in the mouth as either 'light' or 'amusing'!

Nevertheless, he couldn't resist raising his whisky glass in a toast to her as the song came to an end, receiving a narrow-eyed glare in return.

Max grinned in response. He couldn't help himself. Persuading her into a relationship with him was not going to be easy. But he had never backed down from a challenge in his life before, and he wasn't about to start now.

Besides, he might not have had too successful a day but, all things considered, it hadn't been a bad evening so far. If all else failed where January was concerned, he could always fall back on the definite invitation he had received from Josh to attend the family wedding the following Saturday!

CHAPTER THREE

'YOU can't possibly go to the wedding with me next Saturday,' January told Max firmly as she sat down at the table opposite him, the opportunity to tell him exactly this being the only reason she had agreed to have a drink with him at the end of the evening in the first place.

He eyed her with some amusement, blue eyes dark with suppressed laughter. 'Why can't I?' he returned mildly. 'Josh seemed perfectly sincere about the invitation.'

'I'm sure that he was,' January acknowledged disgruntledly, more than a little annoyed with her cousin-in-law-to-be for offhandedly having made the invitation at all. Kissing her as a stag-night bet was one thing, inviting Max to come to the wedding with her was something else entirely. 'It simply isn't possible,' she insisted determinedly.

'Why isn't it?' he prompted softly. 'I didn't get the impression, based on the fact that Josh made the invitation, that you intended going with anyone else,' he added hardly.

'Well, you were wrong,' January told him stubbornly. 'I'm going with my family,' she enlightened impatiently as she saw the way his gaze narrowed speculatively. 'Taking a complete stranger to the wedding with me would be tantamount to making some sort of announcement to the rest of my family,' she added irritably as he returned her gaze blandly now. 'An inappropriate announcement!' She glared her annoyance at his inability not to have seen that in the first place.

He might have shown a marked interest in her the last two evenings, but she was sure he wouldn't want to give either her or her family that particular impression!

'It's a week away, January.' He shrugged. 'A lot can happen in a week,' he added enigmatically.

A lot always 'happened' in her week, her work on the farm and the singing at the hotel in the evenings keeping her more than busy—but this man, with his powerful good looks, and his rich sophistication, simply did *not* 'happen' in that life!

'I said no, Max,' she reiterated firmly. 'And I meant no.' She took a sip of her sparkling water, feeling in need of something a little stronger, but unable to do so when she still had to drive home.

'Whatever,' he dismissed uninterestedly. 'You were good this evening, January,' he changed the subject abruptly. 'Despite having been very soundly kissed in the middle of it,' he added hardly.

'It was a bet, Max.' January sighed, too tired and irritable to simply tell him to mind his own business. 'A stag-night dare,' she enlarged. 'I was at school with most of that group; they thought it a great laugh to dare Josh to kiss me.'

In fact, Peter Meridew had had cause to speak to Josh and several of his friends before the end of the evening, claiming their rowdiness was disturbing the other guests.

Max gave her a look that told her precisely how unfunny he had found the whole incident, too!

Peter Meridew was one thing, but what did it really matter what Max thought? Or said, for that matter. He was a guest at the hotel—for how long, she had no idea—but pretty soon he was going to move on. And when he did, he was not going to leave a broken-hearted singer/farmer behind him!

Because she would be deceiving herself if she didn't admit—inwardly, at least!—that she had found his earlier behaviour, in jumping to her supposed rescue, highly chivalrous. An old-fashioned description, perhaps, but that was exactly how it had seemed at the time. No wonder those ladies of old had swooned into the arms of their saviour! And she didn't doubt for a moment that Max would have carried out his intention to knock Josh to the floor if she hadn't stepped in and explained the situation.

'It's late.' She gave a weary sigh, pushing her long dark hair back over her shoulder, looking over to give John a sympathetic smile as he cleaned the bar prior to his own shift ending for the night. 'I really should be on my way.' She wasn't as late as last night, obviously, but she definitely felt more tired.

More emotional? Possibly. One thing she did know: she had better get herself as far away from Max as possible—now!—or risk giving in to that emotion.

Max gave an inclination of his head, his gaze once more as intense as it had been the previous evening. 'You do look as if you've had enough for one night, would you allow me to order you a taxi?'

She gave a rueful smile. 'There would be little point in that.' Tempting as the offer was to relinquish the hour-long drive into someone else's more than capable hands. 'I don't work tomorrow evening, so it would simply mean another drive out tomorrow to pick up my car.'

'I wouldn't mind picking you up.' Max shrugged.

'That way, you could introduce me to the rest of your family,' he added pointedly.

And that way he would no longer be the 'complete stranger' to them she had accused him of being earlier! Very clever, she acknowledged admiringly—if totally out of the question.

'I don't think so, thanks.' She smiled as she stood up to put an end to the conversation.

Max stood up, too, easily towering over her. 'It really isn't a problem,' he assured her smoothly. 'Besides, John was telling me earlier that you have some sort of stalker in the area…?' He frowned as the two of them gave the barman a friendly wave before walking out into the reception area.

He did have a point there. So far, the Night Striker had only attacked women in quiet, country areas, and while the hotel car park hardly qualified as that it was pretty deserted this time of night…

'Hmm,' she acknowledged with a grimace. 'Six attacks in the last six months.'

Max's eyes darkened at the knowledge. 'Then, if you really do insist on driving yourself home…? That's what I thought,' he acknowledged dryly as she gave an affirmative nod. 'In that case, there is no way I'm going to let you walk out to the car park alone while I go upstairs to my warm and cosy hotel suite.'

'It's quite well lit,' she assured him.

'I still don't feel happy about letting you walk to your car unescorted,' he insisted firmly.

She could see by his determined expression that it would be no use pointing out that it was something she normally did three nights of the week. Every week. That she would do again once he had left the hotel…

'You're starting to sound like my elder sister May

now!' January teased as Max moved to drape her coat around her shoulders in preparation for going outside in the cold winter air.

He gave a start of surprise. 'I'm not sure I like sounding like someone's elder sister!'

January laughed softly. 'Will it help if I tell you I'm very attached to both my sisters?'

'It might,' he conceded slowly. 'Here, let me help you,' he offered as she struggled to put her arms into the sleeves of her coat as the cold wind outside penetrated the thin material of her dress.

Helping her into her coat was good manners, January acknowledged frowningly; allowing his arm to drape casually across her shoulders as they walked over to her car was something else entirely!

Not that she wasn't grateful for the added warmth of his body so close to hers—it was that closeness that bothered her. Disturbed her. Excited her!

She had never met anyone quite like Max before, finding his air of sophistication, his complete air of confidence, those overpoweringly good looks, enticing to say the least.

Admit it, January, she derided herself; you're intrigued by the man, in spite of yourself!

Intrigued? Her heart was pounding, her pulse racing, the flush that warmed her cheeks owing nothing to the cold and everything to Max's proximity.

'I really wasn't meaning to sound insulting just now when I likened your concern to my elder sister's.' She burst into speech in an effort to hide the confused emotions welling up inside her. 'I—it was rather—endearing,' she added awkwardly, at the same time glancing across to where her car was parked, quickly gauging how much longer it was going to take to reach it. Not long now, thank goodness. 'As the youngest of three, I've always come in for the biggest amount of sisterly advice. Even March sometimes gets in on the act.' She grimaced. 'And she's known as the more impetuous one of us!'

'January. March. And May,' Max repeated slowly. 'Three months of the year,' he added speculatively.

'Oh, that's easily explained.' January came to a grateful halt beside her little car, at the same time searching in her bag for her keys. 'You see—'

'All I can see at the moment, January, is the most beautiful woman I have ever set eyes on,' Max cut in harshly. 'It's all I've been able to see for the last thirty-six hours!'

January looked up at him sharply, becoming suddenly still as she found herself drowning in the fathomless depths of his eyes.

'January!' he groaned throatily even as his head lowered and his lips claimed hers, at the same time as his arms moved about the slenderness of her waist to pull her close to the warm hardness of his body.

Drowning must be something like this, January guessed dreamily a few minutes later; the initial fight against the inevitable, before the complete surrender to a force of such strength it was impossible to fight it any longer.

She knew nothing about this man but the little he had told her—the little he had chosen to tell her. She didn't even know his surname, she realized with a shocked jolt, and yet—

She couldn't think any more, couldn't formulate two words together in her brain, could only breathe and feel Max, her body on fire with the desire his kisses engendered.

Her arms moved up to his shoulders as she held on to him, one of her hands becoming enmeshed in the dark thickness of his hair, that hair silky to the touch.

Max groaned low in his throat, evidence of his own pleasure at her touch, his mouth moving more fiercely against hers now as he deepened the kiss, his tongue moving searchingly over the sensitivity of her inner lip before probing deeper.

January had never felt such oneness with another person before, as if she were a part of Max, and he a part of her, having no idea any more where Max began and she ended.

It was—

Tiny pinpoints of icy cold were falling against the warmth of her face, January's eyes opening wide in puzzlement as the unwanted intrusion persisted, blinking dazedly as she looked up to see the snow gently falling down on them.

Max broke the kiss reluctantly, his arms remaining firmly about her waist as he gave a rueful grimace at the steadily falling snowflakes. 'Almost as good as a cold shower,' he murmured self-derisively, his gaze warm as he turned back to January. 'Probably as well,' he conceded ruefully. 'I would like the first time I make love to you to be somewhere a little more—comfortable than a hotel car park!'

The first time…? That statement implied it would only be the first time of many…!

January pulled gently out of his arms, turned away to hide her confusion, determinedly turning her attention to a renewed search in her handbag for her car keys. Where on earth were they? What—?

'January…?' Max reached out a hand to lift up her

chin, his gaze becoming searching as he saw the paleness of her face.

'I really do have to go now, Max,' she told him awkwardly, sighing her relief as she at last located her keys at the bottom of her bag. 'It's very late—'

'Or early,' he put in lightly. 'Depends on your point of view, doesn't it?' he teased. 'I want to see you again, January,' he told her firmly. 'Tomorrow,' he added determinedly. 'Will you have lunch with me?'

Would she? Could she? *Dared* she?

Because she was in no doubt that if she agreed to see this man again there would be a repeat of the kisses they had just shared, that the next time there might be no pulling back—that even now her body still burned for the touch of his!

But could she not see Max again? Could she just walk away from him, from the totally new emotions she had known just now in his arms, and calmly get on with the rest of her life? Could she do that? Did she want to do that?

'Lunch tomorrow would be nice,' she accepted huskily, not quite able to meet his gaze now, afraid that he might be able to see the hunger still burning in her eyes if she did. A hunger that seemed to consume every part of her…

'Nice isn't quite the way I would have put it.' Max's mouth twisted ruefully. 'But I suppose it will have to do,' he accepted self-derisively. 'Are you going to be okay driving home in this weather?' He frowned up at the snow that was falling more heavily than ever.

What was the alternative? To stay the night with him in his hotel suite? Somehow she didn't think so! She might respond to this man in a way that was totally new—and a little frightening?—to her, but that didn't mean she was about to fall willingly into his arms at the first opportunity.

'I'll be fine,' she dismissed, willing her hand not to shake as she unlocked her car door. 'This is the north of England, Max; it often snows here. If you allowed your life to be dictated by the weather you would never do anything,' she assured him.

'Okay,' he agreed with obvious reluctance. 'Where shall we meet for lunch?' he prompted as January got into her car.

She looked up at him. 'How about here? At twelve-thirty? There's a nice pub a couple of miles away where they serve a great Sunday lunch.' Working at the hotel, she did not want to be seen by Peter Meridew eating lunch here with one of the guests. Especially a guest like Max!

'Okay.' Max nodded slowly, bending down so that he filled the doorway, making it impossible for January to close the car door. 'You won't change your mind?' he prompted huskily.

She already had—several times! But, no…she wouldn't change her mind.

'I'll be here at twelve-thirty,' she promised, giving an involuntary shiver as the piercing wind and snow entered the car. 'Brr.' She grimaced pointedly.

'Sorry,' Max murmured ruefully, stepping back so that she could close the car door.

January wound down the window. 'You should get inside,' she advised lightly, grateful when her car started the first time she turned the key; it was an old car, and prone to letting her down at inconvenient moments. 'You're getting very wet!' As were his tailored suit and expensive-looking leather shoes.

Now where had she—?

'I'll wait here until you've driven off, if you don't mind,' Max told her grimly. 'It's the least I can do!'

He so obviously wasn't accustomed to having his wishes overridden in this way that January couldn't help but smile. 'I'll see you tomorrow,' she told him as she drove off with a wave of her hand.

She passed John on his way to his own car as she drove out of the car park, giving him a friendly wave too before accelerating out onto the deserted road.

She would be lying if she said it was an easy drive home, because it was far from that, the drive on the untarmacked cart-track that led up to the farm the worst part of it. But at last she arrived in the farmyard, relieved to switch off the car engine and get out of the car, flexing the tension from her tired shoulder muscles.

Tension not just caused from the difficult drive home, January conceded ruefully. There was Max, her response to him, to worry about, too.

But the tension left her completely as she stood looking at the surrounding countryside, at the snow-covered hills, slowly becoming filled with an inner peace. The land, as far as her eye could see, belonged to them. It might be a tough life sometimes, a lot of hard work, often with no obvious return, the weather and circumstances unkind to them occasionally, too, but it was all theirs.

Nothing—and no one—was ever going to change that…

She was late for their luncheon appointment, by precisely ten minutes, Max realized, scowling after yet another glance at his gold wrist-watch as he strolled restlessly up and down the reception area of the hotel.

Always a stickler for being on time for appointments

himself, Max found January's tardiness doubly frustrating. Firstly, because of that abhorrence of lateness in others as much as in himself; secondly—the fact that January hadn't arrived at twelve-thirty, as she had said she would, might mean that she wasn't coming at all!

It was that second reason that was the most frustrating.

Maybe he had come on a little strong with her again last night? Maybe he shouldn't have kissed her quite that passionately?

But once he'd held January in his arms, not to have kissed her in the way he had had been totally beyond his control. In truth, he had wanted to do a lot more than just kiss her!

Her body had been warm and fluid, her breasts pressed invitingly against his chest, her thighs moulding perfectly against his; it had taken every ounce of his will-power not to sweep her off her feet and carry her up to his hotel room. Where he had wanted to explore every delectable inch of her body with his hands and lips!

Stop it, Max, he instructed himself firmly. Wasn't it enough that he had spent a sleepless night, initially worrying in case she hadn't got home safely, and wishing that he had asked her to call him when she'd got in, followed by a hunger just for sight or touch of January, without repeating that discomfort now? He couldn't remember the last time he had hungered for a woman in this way—if he ever had!—let alone got up in the middle of the night to take a cold shower in an effort to deal with the problem.

He glanced at his watch again. She was fifteen minutes late now—

'Er—sir? Mr Golding, isn't it?'

He turned to scowl in acknowledgement as the receptionist called hesitantly across to him.

'I believe there's a telephone call for you.' She pointed to the telephone at the end of the desk, the flashing light indicating the call.

Probably Jude, checking up on progress, Max realized frowningly as he moved to take the call. Just what he needed at this precise moment!

'Yes?' he snapped into the receiver.

'Max?' January returned uncertainly.

He willed himself to relax, not to show how angry he was—and failed miserably. 'Where the hell are you?' he rasped; the fact that she was telephoning him at all meant that she wasn't on her way here—or, in fact, intending to be!

'Well, at the moment I'm at home—'

'You should be here!' he snapped, his hand tightly gripping the receiver.

'But until a short time ago I was sitting in my car in a ditch,' January continued, determined. 'Max, I'm sorry,' she added huskily.

'I really am. I set out in plenty of time to get there at twelve-thirty, but the car skidded on some ice, I lost control, and—well, I ended up in the ditch. I telephoned as soon as I could—'

'Are you hurt?' Max cut in sharply, furious with himself now for having lost his temper with her initially. If she were hurt—! That possibility didn't bear thinking about!

'Just a little bump on the head,' January dismissed. 'But the car is probably a write-off—'

'Forget the car,' he cut in. 'It's easily replaceable. You aren't.'

'Well it might be easily replaceable to you.' She

laughed ruefully. 'I'm not in such a healthy financial position, I'm afraid. But never mind that,' she changed the subject. 'There is no way I'm going to make it for lunch now, so could we make it dinner this evening, instead? March says she doesn't need her car this evening, so I can borrow that. As long as I promise not to put that in a ditch, too,' she added dryly.

Max's head was still full of horrifying visions of the first time she had landed in a ditch, at how nearly he had lost her, when he had only just found her!

'Wouldn't it be easier if I were to pick you up?' he suggested tautly. 'That way, if anyone ends up in a ditch, it will be me!'

'No, that won't do at all,' she came back instantly.

'January, could you just forget this idea you have that my meeting your family is tantamount to an engagement announcement,' he interrupted impatiently, 'and just look at the safety aspect instead? I do not want—'

'Max, this has nothing to do with what my family may or may not think—' The embarrassment could be heard in her voice '—and everything to do with the fact that I live in a very remote area, high up in the hills. Trying to direct you there would be a nightmare.'

In that case, the thought of her driving down to him was a nightmare, too—for him. He—

'Maybe we should just forget meeting up at all,' January continued evenly. 'The weather seems to be against us, and—'

'No!' Max cut in tautly. 'No, January, to me not seeing you today is not an option.' He simply couldn't go through another night like last night!

'To me, either,' she came back softly.

So softly, Max wasn't sure he had heard her correctly, or whether it was just wishful thinking on his part. The former, he hoped!

'Okay, dinner,' he accepted huskily. 'Here. At seven-thirty.'

'Fine,' she agreed breathlessly. 'Oh, before you go, Max, there is just one little thing…' she added teasingly.

'Yes?' he prompted warily, feeling his tension rising once again.

'Don't you think it might be helpful if I were to know your surname?' she asked playfully. 'It was a little embarrassing a few minutes ago when I telephoned and had to ask Patty if there could possibly be an irate-looking guest pacing up and down in Reception—because I had no idea how to ask for you by name!'

That thought hadn't even occurred to him. But, now that he thought of it, he didn't know her surname either; it hadn't seemed important at the time.

It still wasn't important; she was January to him, the woman he wanted with a fierceness that was totally consuming his every waking thought. Although he could see her point…

'Golding,' he supplied laughingly. 'Maxim Patrick Golding.'

Complete silence on the other end of the telephone line followed his announcement. A sudden, tense silence.

'January…?' he prompted as the seconds slowly passed with only that silence on the other end of the telephone line.

'Did you say Golding?' she finally asked in a hushed voice.

'Yes, I did,' Max returned warily. 'January—'

'*You're* M. P. Golding?' Her voice rose disbelievingly.

Max's hand tightened about the telephone receiver. Something was wrong. Very, very wrong. 'I just told you I am,' he confirmed slowly, having no idea what the problem was with his name. Only knowing that there obviously was one.

Why had January repeated his name in that formal way, M. P. Golding, as if he were the author of a book, or—? Or…!

'January, what's your own surname?' he prompted with a wince of foreboding.

'With first names like January, March and May? I'm sure, if you try, you can work that one out for yourself, Mr Golding! If there's really any need for you to do so!' she added scathingly. 'Goodbye!'

'January—' Max broke off abruptly, realizing as he heard the clatter of the receiver being slammed down on the other end of the line that he was talking to himself.

Max slowly replaced his own receiver, the colour draining from his cheeks as the truth hit him with the force of a sledgehammer. January, March, and May. All months of the year. All months in the Gregorian calendar.

Calendar…

It was all too much of a coincidence, January having two sisters, their names all months of the year; January's surname *had* to be Calendar!

Damn, damn, damn!

CHAPTER FOUR

'JANUARY, where on earth are you going?' May demanded incredulously as she followed her outside.

January didn't even pause in her long strides across the yard. 'To get my car out of the ditch, of course,' she dismissed impatiently.

'But there's no hurry to do that until the weather improves,' May protested reasoningly as January climbed into the cab of the tractor. 'After all, you said it's probably a write-off, anyway.' Her sister grimaced.

It probably was, the whole of the front wing on the driver's side of the car seeming to have concertinaed into itself as it hit the other side of the ditch.

But it had at least stopped snowing, and January needed something to do, desperately needed to keep herself physically busy in an effort to stop herself from thinking too much. From thinking at all, if possible!

M. P. Golding! She had recognized the name instantly, clearly remembered it as the signature of the lawyer at the bottom of the letter they had received before Christmas—from the Marshall Corporation, offering to buy their farm. The same name of the lawyer who had visited the farm yesterday and spoken to May on the same subject…?

January still couldn't believe it! Couldn't stop thinking of it, no matter how much she tried…

'It can't just stay there, May,' she insisted grimly.

'It can stay there for a couple of days, until the snow clears a little,' her sister insisted.

January gave a firm shake of her head. 'I'm going now.'

'January, what's happened?' May looked at her concernedly. 'You were bright and bubbly this morning, before the accident. Perhaps that bump on the head was more serious than we initially thought. Perhaps we should call Dr. Young—'

'I don't need a doctor, May.' Not that sort of doctor, anyway! She forced herself to relax slightly, turning to smile at her sister. 'It's just a bump,' she insisted lightly—the throbbing pain at her temple was nothing compared to the one in her heart. And a medical doctor could do nothing to cure that! 'Look, I'll just drive down and see if it's possible to tow the car out of the ditch,' she offered as a compromise. 'The fresh air will probably do me good,' she added encouragingly.

May still didn't look convinced, frowning up at her concernedly. 'Aren't you supposed to be going out again later this evening?'

January blinked, no longer able to hold her sister's gaze. 'Change of plan,' she dismissed. 'Look, it's cold out here, why don't you go back inside?' she suggested with an encouraging smile. 'I promise I won't be long.'

'Okay,' May sighed. 'I'll have a mug of hot tea waiting for you when you get back.'

January gave an inner sigh of relief at her sister's belated capitulation, starting the noisy tractor engine before giving her sister a friendly wave and driving out of the farmyard.

She just needed some time to herself. Time to work out exactly what had been happening the last couple of days. Time to consider exactly what Max Golding had been doing the last couple of days!

Because, despite what he had said before she'd

abruptly ended their telephone conversation, she couldn't help thinking that he had to have known all the time that she was one of the Calendar sisters.

Was that the real reason he had shown such a marked interest in her? Had it all been some sort of devious plan on his part, to divide the sisters and, in doing so, perhaps conquer?

That was her worst fear, the dread that held her in partial shock at the realization of exactly who he was. Because last night, as the two of them had kissed, January had known that she was falling in love with Max, that perhaps she already was in love with him.

He was like no other man she had ever known, was possessed of a self-confidence that was totally reassuring, was obviously intelligent, as well as sophisticated, his wealth beyond question.

She had simply been swept off her feet by him!

But was she *meant* to have been? That was the question that plagued her battered and bruised heart.

One thing she knew for certain: once he had had time to think this thing through, it wouldn't take Max too long to make an appearance at the farm. Which was another good reason for her to make herself scarce from the farm as much as possible over the next few days.

Although that didn't appear much of a likelihood as she turned the tractor round a sharp bend in the snow-covered track and found a car creeping slowly along from the other direction, blocking her own way in the process, the person behind the steering wheel visibly Max Golding!

January braked so sharply to avoid actually driving into him that the tractor instantly came to a shuddering halt, Max obviously breaking at the same time, the wheels on his car not having quite the same traction as the vehicle skidded slightly but didn't quite go off the track.

January stared at him in absolute horror; the last thing she had expected was that Max would actually drive out to the farm almost immediately after she had so abruptly terminated their telephone call. She had thought she had some hours to gather her own scattered defences, possibly twenty-four hours if Max needed the same time to think that she did.

But as he climbed out of the car she realized how wrong she had been. He was no longer wearing the 'tailored suit and handmade shoes' that May had taken such glee in watching him get muddy yesterday—and that had struck such a chord with January last night when she'd thought of them. Now he was dressed in a thick blue sweater and denims, heavy hiking boots to protect his feet—obviously he had learnt his lesson about suitable clothing for visiting a working farm the previous day!

Her fingers clenched about the steering wheel as he approached the tractor, his expression grim. What was he going to say to her? What were they going to say to each other?

Attack is better than defence, she remembered her father once telling them, pushing open the cab door to climb down onto the running-board before lowering herself down into the snow, her head back challengingly as she waited for Max to reach her side.

'I didn't know, January,' came his first abrupt comment.

She gave a humourless smile. 'Didn't know what, Mr Golding?' she scorned. 'That my surname is Calendar? That I'm one of the three sisters who owns the farm the corporation you work for is trying to buy out? Forgive me if I find that a little hard to believe!' she derided hardly.

And she did find it hard. It seemed too much of a coincidence that Max should turn out to be the lawyer who had sent that initial letter on behalf of the big American corporation he obviously worked for. That he was the same man who had visited May on the farm yesterday. The same man who was trying to persuade them into selling the farm.

Too much of a coincidence, in those circumstances, that the two of them should have met at all. Even allowing for such a coincidence, it was doubly hard to believe that Max would have made such a beeline for her in the way that he had if it weren't for the fact that he already knew she was one of the sisters who was proving so intractable to the financial offers he was making on behalf of the Marshall Corporation.

Max's expression was grim. 'I can't help what you believe, I can only repeat that until a short time ago I genuinely had no idea what your surname was, or who you are.'

And she could only repeat—inwardly, at least—that she didn't believe him!

She gave him another scathing glance. 'What are you doing here, Mr Golding? I'm sure my sister May has already made it more than plain that we aren't interested—'

'Will you stop calling me by my surname in that contemptuous way?' he protested irritably. 'It was Max before. And I'm still Max.'

Not in the same way, he wasn't. He was the enemy now. The known enemy. Untrustworthy. Worse, he was devious.

'And, yes, your sister May did make it quite clear to me yesterday that you aren't interested in selling the farm,' he continued impatiently. 'Now that I know of the family connection, the likeness between the two of you, apart from the colour of your eyes, is quite remarkable,' he allowed heavily. 'I simply wasn't looking for that likeness when I visited the farm yesterday.'

'No?' January derided disbelievingly. 'Then you're going to get even more of a shock when—or if!—you meet March; ''like three peas in a pod'', our father used to say about us,' she told him dismissively.

'I said there was a likeness, January; the way you look, the sound of your voice, is utterly unique,' he assured her evenly.

Her mouth twisted humourlessly. 'Of course it is,' she humoured scathingly. 'Well, if you wouldn't mind moving your vehicle out of my way; some of us have work to do.'

Max looked at her closely, a frown between his eyes as his gaze narrowed. 'Is that bump on your head from the accident earlier?'

Her gloved hand moved up instinctively to cover the discolouration at her temple. She would be lying if she claimed that it didn't hurt, because it did; she just had no intention of discussing her injury—or her inner pain—with Max Golding!

'January?' he prompted sharply.

'Yes, it is,' she confirmed dismissively. 'If you turn your car around in the gateway just behind you—'

'January, I am not interested in discussing turning the car around,' he bit out in fiercely measured tones.

Her eyes flashed a warning. 'Well, I'm not interested in discussing anything else with you—which pretty well leaves us with nothing left to say to each other!' She turned back to the tractor.

Only to have her arm clasped between steely fingers as Max swung her back round to face him.

'I have several things I want to say to you,' he told her forcefully, blue eyes glittering dangerously. 'Firstly, I repeat my claim that I had no idea of your connection with the Calendar farm—'

'And I repeat that I don't believe you!' she came back harshly.

Max became suddenly still, his eyes so pale a blue now they looked almost grey. 'I don't tell lies, January,' he bit out coldly. 'Have you seen a doctor about that bump on the head?' he changed the subject frowningly.

Her mouth twisted contemptuously. 'Careful, you're starting to sound like May again!'

His mouth tightened at her deliberate barb. 'If she's as concerned about you as I am then I think I like your elder sister.'

January's cheeks became angrily flushed as she gave a humourless smile. 'I very much doubt the sentiment is reciprocated!'

Max shook his head. 'I'm not out to win popularity contests, I'm only interested in making sure you've suffered no ill effects from the accident—'

'The only "ill effects" I have are from having to look at you any longer than I need to!' January told him insultingly, at last managing to pull her arm out of his grasp as she glared up at him. 'Now, are you going to move your car, or do I have to go round you by taking the tractor into one of the fields?' she challenged hardly.

Move, she pleaded inwardly. Just move. If only so

that she could get away from his overwhelming presence. Because if he didn't soon move, she was very much afraid she was going to cry!

At the moment, her only defence against her feelings for this man was her anger. And she wasn't sure how much longer she would be able to maintain it.

Max stared at her frustratedly. She was, without doubt, the most stubborn, most determined—

More stubborn than he was? More determined than he was? Somehow he didn't think so.

At the moment, January was furiously angry with him for what she thought of as his deception. He could see only too clearly that nothing he said or did just now—or in the immediate future, for that matter—was going to change her feelings for him. Besides, he was in something of a quandary himself, had always made it a rule to keep his private and business life completely separate. That way there was never any question of a conflict of interest.

January Calendar. Of all the women he could have found himself so attracted to, it had to be one of the Calendar sisters!

What were the chances of that happening? Really? Almost nil, he would have said, with the farm being such a distance away from the hotel. That little mischief called Fate, he felt, was playing some sort of game with him.

But he had challenged Fate before, and won; he could win this time, too. If he still wanted to…

That was the real problem here. He had been stunned to learn that January was one of the three Calendar sisters he had been sent here to persuade into selling their farm. More than stunned. In truth, he simply didn't know what to do about it. A most unusual occurrence for him.

'You won't agree to see a doctor about that bump on the head?' He tried one last time to make her see sense about that at least.

'No, I won't,' she came back predictably.

His mouth tightened even as he gave an acknowledging nod of his head; stubborn didn't even begin to describe this particular woman!

'I take it our date for dinner this evening is also cancelled?' he prompted dryly.

Her eyes flashed deeply grey. 'You take it correct!' she snapped.

'I thought so,' he murmured mildly. 'As I obviously no longer have any other plans for today, and as I'm already halfway there already, I may as well drive up the rest of the way to the farm and have another talk to your sisters.'

January's eyes widened incredulously at this suggestion. 'You will be wasting your time!'

He shrugged. 'It's my time to waste.'

Her mouth twisted scathingly. 'I thought your time belonged to the Marshall Corporation?'

It was true that the Marshall Corporation had become the main part of his life for almost fifteen years, that his hours of work weren't the usual nine to five, Monday to Friday of a lawyer in a normal law practice. But with no family ties to speak of, only an apartment in London that he rarely visited to actually call home, that had never particularly bothered Max. In fact, he had welcomed the long hours of work and travel that were often necessary in his job.

In the circumstances, hearing January casting aspersions on that particular aspect of his life was not something he welcomed!

'Even I have weekends and holiday off, January,' he snapped, knowing, even as he made the claim, that it wasn't strictly accurate.

He could probably count the number of holidays he had taken the last fifteen years on the fingers of one hand. But holidays had never seemed important to him, were often an inconvenient interruption to business. Besides, he visited such exotic places during his business travels that holidays weren't really necessary.

'You were still working on New Year's Eve,' January reminded tauntingly.

His mouth tightened at her obvious implication. She still believed he had deliberately singled her out that evening, that it was all a part of some elaborate plan on his part to gain control of the Calendar farm.

But there was no way he would have deliberately planned to meet January in that way, certainly not to have been completely knocked off his feet by her in the way he had been. It was simply an unwritten rule with him never to mix business with pleasure.

Not that he thought there was much chance of him doing that now, either!

Oh, he was still attracted to January, in a way he had probably never been to any other woman, but there were two ways of looking at the fact she had turned out to be one of the Calendar sisters. The first way meant that he now had an uphill struggle ahead of him if he were to continue his personal pursuit of her. The second way was as a timely intervention, Fate not playing games with him at all, but instead stepping in to stop him from making the biggest mistake of his life.

Damn it, he liked his life the way it was: completely

uncomplicated by personal ties! And there was no way, now, that he could have an enjoyable, but brief, relationship with January.

He drew in a deeply controlling breath. 'I'll back my car up and let you past,' he told her evenly.

Her eyes widened at his unexpected capitulation. 'You're still wasting your time going up to the farm,' she assured him hardly. 'My sisters aren't interested in selling any more than I am.'

He gave another shrug. 'If that's the case, it will cease to be my problem and become someone else's.' He hoped!

She gave him a guarded look. 'Are you threatening us?'

'Not in the least!' He gave an exasperated shake of his head. 'January, no one can force any of you into selling if you're really not interested in doing so.'

But even as he said the words he knew that wasn't strictly true; Jude wasn't a man used to hearing the word no, let alone actually taking any notice of it. And he wanted the land the Calendar farm stood on pretty badly...

January didn't look any more convinced of his sincerity than he had actually making the claim, that guarded look having turned to one of wariness now.

'It's cold out here, January,' he added briskly, not quite meeting her searching gaze now. 'I'll back up and let you continue on your way. Your car is a mess, by the way,' he added hardly, having driven past the car in the ditch on his way up here, wincing as he imagined January behind the wheel as she lost control and crashed. Worse, that she had been driving to meet him at the time it had happened...

Not that he thought that would happen again;

January had made it more than obvious the last ten minutes or so that she would never agree to meet him again, for dinner or anything else!

Cut your losses and move on, Max, he mentally advised himself determinedly. Goodness knew he had done it often enough in the past, never in the same place long enough to allow himself to become too attached to any woman. Or them to him. January Calendar was no different, he told himself firmly. Only the force of his attraction to her was different…

All the more reason to get as far away from here as he could, as quickly as he could!

Except Jude seemed to have other ideas on the subject, Max discovered later that afternoon when he returned to the hotel, after a frustrating hour spent at the Calendar farm with May and March Calendar, to put a call through to his boss and friend.

'You can't have put our case strongly enough,' Jude drawled unsympathetically. 'How difficult can it be to persuade three old maids that they would be better off living in a nice bungalow somewhere than working their fingers to the bone on a hill farm that simply doesn't, and never will, pay for itself?'

'Three old maids', indeed! Max could easily predict the reaction of any of the three undoubtedly beautiful sisters to being called that! It had been interesting to meet the third sister, March, when he'd got to the farm, to see the physical similarity between all three sisters. Although March, he had quickly learnt, was the most tempestuous of the three, telling him in no uncertain terms exactly what he, and the Marshall Corporation, could do with their offer to buy the Calendar property. May had been a little politer, but her answer had still been the same as that of her siblings.

But for some reason Max didn't actually want to correct Jude in his mistake concerning the age of the three sisters, didn't want to give the other man the opportunity to perhaps put two and two together and come up with four, to question the reason for Max's own reluctance to pursue this thing any further.

'They were born there, Jude,' he repeated March's indignant remark of earlier. 'The family has lived there for generations—'

'Max, are you going soft on me?' Jude cut in disbelievingly.

As well he might. He and Jude had been at school together, had lost touch for a while when attending different universities, but Jude had sought Max out several years later when his business empire had begun to expand, easily persuading Max to become his personal and company lawyer. It was a decision that Max had never regretted. Until today…

'No, of course not,' he dismissed harshly. 'I just—'

'You just…?' Jude prompted speculatively.

'Leave it with me for a few more days, okay?' he answered impatiently, willing himself to relax as his hand tightly gripped the receiver—so much for his earlier decision to tell Jude to just cut and run over this proposed deal. So that he could cut and run himself! 'How are you doing with the beautiful April?' he prompted tautly.

'Changing the subject, Max?' Jude guessed shrewdly.

That was the problem with Jude: he was too astute. And the last thing Max wanted was for the other man to even begin to guess at the emotional tangle Max now found himself in.

Part of him wanted to just pass the problem of the

Calendar farm over to someone else, and in the process get himself as far away from January as he possibly could—something that he now knew he needed to do. But the professional side of him, the part of him that had been loyal to Jude and the Marshall Corporation for the last fifteen years, decreed that he had to continue trying to talk the Calendar sisters into selling their birthright.

'Not particularly,' he came back easily. 'I merely wondered if you had been any more successful with April than I was,' he added dryly.

'Not in the least,' Jude came back cheerfully. 'She insists on treating me as if I'm nothing more to her than a naughty little brother.'

'Novel.' Max grinned at the thought of the arrogantly successful Jude being cast in such an unflattering role.

The other man chuckled. 'Actually, I'm quite enjoying it. She really is a fascinating woman,' he added appreciatively.

Nowhere near as fascinating, to Max, as January had proved to be! But at least he had veered the other man off the subject of the Calendar sisters, which was, after all, what he had set out to do by introducing the subject of April Robine.

'To get back to the Calendar farm,' Jude continued determinedly—proof that, as usual, he hadn't been veered off the subject at all! 'We really need to get that settled and out of the way in the next few weeks, so that we can get on with drawing up the plans. Offer them more money if nothing else works,' he added hardly.

Dogged. Single-minded. They were qualities in Jude that he had always admired in the past. But where this particular problem was concerned Max found those traits extremely irritating.

'I'm well aware of the time-scale involved, Jude,' he snapped. 'But I don't think, in this case, that the offer of more money is going to make the slightest bit of difference.'

In fact, Max was sure that it wouldn't. The offer already made was far above the market value of the property, and despite the fact that the Calendar sisters obviously weren't exactly wealthy, none of them had been in the least tempted to accept the offer. Money, it seemed, just wasn't important to them.

'I really don't want to have to come over there myself, Max,' Jude said softly.

Max didn't want the other man to come here himself, either. For one thing, it implied failure on his part if Jude had to deal with this himself. For another, he simply didn't want Jude coming here, meeting the three sisters, putting that two and two together, and realizing that Max's real problem was January!

It seemed that, unless he wanted to admit the truth to Jude, that he had unwittingly become personally involved with January, one of the Calendar sisters, something he would rather not do, he really had no choice but to stay here and continue the negotiations on Jude's behalf.

'I asked you to leave it with me a few days longer,' he reminded the other man harshly.

'A few more days is all you have, Max,' Jude conceded warningly before abruptly ending the call.

Max slowly replaced his own receiver before turning to stare frustratedly out of the window of his hotel room, the snow once again falling outside not helping the darkness of his mood. What a damned mess!

There was obviously no way Jude was going to back down from buying the Calendar farm. Which meant that Max couldn't either.

But how to persuade the Calendar sisters into changing their minds was the problem. Having now met all of them, an insurmountable one, as far as he could see.

But nowhere near as insurmountable as the problem January had become to him personally.

Indulging in an affair with her for the time he was in the area had seemed like a pleasant way to spend his free time. The fact that she had turned out to be one of the reasons he was here at all completely changed that. Besides, having got to know January a little better, having met her sisters, he now knew that January was not the type of woman to have an affair. With anyone.

But least of all him.

Whereas he knew he still wanted her with a fierceness that took his breath away, that everything about her fascinated him: the way she moved, the way she talked, everything!

CHAPTER FIVE

'EXACTLY what do you think you're playing at?' January demanded without preamble the moment Max opened the door of his hotel suite to her insistent knock.

To give him his due, he looked momentarily taken aback by her unexpected appearance, although that surprise was quickly masked as he looked down at her with mocking enquiry. 'Changed your mind about our dinner date?' he drawled dryly.

Her eyes flashed a warning. 'I've changed my mind about nothing concerning you, Mr Golding,' she snapped. 'Absolutely nothing!' she repeated as she pushed past him into the sitting-room of the hotel suite, turning to glare at him when she reached the centre of the room.

He slowly closed the door before strolling in to join her. 'You seem a little—agitated?' he prompted lightly.

Agitated? She was blazing! In fact, she was in such a heated temper that she really didn't need the added warmth of her blue anorak, or the gloves and scarf she had earlier pulled on with it.

'Did you have to tell my sisters that the two of us had already met?' she challenged accusingly. 'Yes, of course you did,' she scathingly answered her own question before he even had chance to do so. 'It was all part of the plan, wasn't it?' she said disgustedly. 'All part of that—'

'Stop right there, January,' he cut in softly—although one glance at the grimness of his features was enough to tell January that his tone was deceptive, that he was now actually as angry as she was, he just showed it in a different way! 'You appear to be—upset,' he allowed evenly. 'And I'm sorry for that. But, at the same time, I also think you are becoming slightly paranoid about this situation—'

'Paranoid!' January echoed disbelievingly. 'Is it "paranoid" when my sisters are absolutely stunned that I somehow forgot to mention that I had already met the lawyer Max Golding? That I was actually supposed to be going out on a date with the man this evening!' she added disgustedly.

She didn't add that he was also the man she had allowed to kiss her so passionately yesterday evening. Or that he was also the man she had been falling in love with!

May and March had been far from happy when January had finally arrived home—minus the car; it really was stuck fast in the ditch. Because somewhere, during the course of their conversation with Max this afternoon, he had let drop the fact that he and January had already met!

To say her sisters had demanded an explanation for January's previous oversight would be putting it mildly. The fact that they had both calmed down once she'd told them exactly what had happened, that they were now just as suspicious of Max's motives as she was, didn't alter the fact that Max had deliberately put her in that defensive position in the first place.

Max gave a shake of his head. 'January, so far I'm not having such a good day myself, so do you think we could just sit down and talk about this like two reasonable adults?' he prompted hardly.

'That may be a little difficult—when only one of us is reasonable!' she came back scathingly.

She would never forget the way her sisters had looked at her on her return this afternoon, could still see that uncertainty in their expressions as they'd waited for her explanation. Oh, she didn't doubt for a moment that they had both believed her explanation, that she was completely innocent in the whole matter, it was only when she'd gone up to her room to change out of her damp clothing that she had decided not to waste another minute before telling Max Golding just how underhand and devious she thought him to be.

He shrugged. 'I'm not even going to ask which one of us you consider that to be,' he returned dryly. 'Although,' he continued firmly as she would have snapped a reply, 'I think the fact that you've driven out here, in the middle of yet another snowstorm, rather negates your being eligible for the description!' he added hardly, blue gaze disapproving.

January opened her mouth a second time to give him that sharp reply, and then changed her mind as her gaze drifted past him to the window, where the snow could be seen falling heavier than ever.

To be honest, she hadn't really noticed the snow falling as she'd driven to the hotel, had been so angry, so consumed with all the things she was going to say to Max, going over and over inside her head the conversation that she intended having with him, that she had driven to the hotel on automatic. So much so she hadn't been aware of the snow!

'January, could you come down off your high horse long enough for us to talk?' Max cajoled softly. 'I'll order us a pot of coffee, and you can drink a warming cup of it while we talk. How about that?'

She wanted to say no, to tell him what he could do with his cup of warm coffee, but now that she was no longer as consumed by burning anger she was able to feel the chill that went all the way through to her bones.

That still wasn't a good enough reason to have coffee with the enemy, a little voice chastened inside her head.

No, it wasn't, she accepted heavily. The truth of the matter was, now that she was here with Max, her anger spent for the most part, she was once again becoming aware of the attraction she felt towards him—still felt towards him, in spite of everything!

Fool, she admonished herself disgustedly. Idiot, she added for good measure.

'January?' Max prompted huskily.

She gave a weary sigh. 'Order your pot of coffee, Max,' she conceded. 'But nothing you have to say is going to change my mind about you. Or the Marshall Corporation,' she added hardly.

He gave an abrupt inclination of his head, moving to the telephone to call Room Service and order the coffee.

January was glad of the few moments' respite from his probing blue gaze, moving away to take off her scarf and gloves before shaking her hair loose from the collar of her jacket.

What was she doing here? Really doing here? Because she had already done what she'd come here to do—and now she was staying to have coffee with the man.

She bit her lip, knowing exactly why she was still here. She couldn't believe—part of her didn't want to believe!—Max was actually guilty of the things she had accused him of!

Not that she had any intention of letting Max see that particular weakness; that wouldn't do at all. She just wanted to see—needed to see—some sort of redeeming feature in his character that told her she was justified to feel about him the way that she really did.

'It's on its way.' Max spoke softly behind her.

Too close behind her, she discovered when she spun round sharply, stepping back as she found Max standing only inches away from her.

He looked at her quizzically. 'You were miles away.'

'Wishing myself…' she came back tautly.

He gave a pained wince. 'Then that makes two of us,' he murmured huskily. 'I was wishing the same thing a short time ago,' he explained at her questioning look.

January's breath caught in her throat at the burning intensity of his gaze. 'And now?'

'Now?' he echoed with a self-derisive grimace. 'Now I wish it would just keep snowing. Snowing. And snowing. I wish, January—' he took a step closer to her '—that the rest of the world would just go away, that the two of us could get marooned alone together in here. For a week. A month!' he concluded heavily.

She looked up at him uncertainly, her breath now coming in short, shallow gasps. 'Can you get snowed in in a hotel room?' she breathed huskily.

'Probably not,' he conceded ruefully. 'But—' He broke off as a knock sounded on the door. 'That will be the coffee,' he acknowledged disgustedly.

'So much for being marooned alone together,' January pointed out softly.

He gave a derisive inclination of his head. 'Maybe that wasn't such a good idea, after all,' he rasped before moving abruptly away to open the door and admit the maid with their tray of coffee.

He seemed different this evening, January acknowledged frowningly. Apart from that brief lapse just now, he was more distant. More remote. His gaze no longer burning with that intensity, but wary.

Of course he was different, she instantly admonished herself; his cover was blown, which meant he no longer needed to act like a man who was besotted with her.

'Cream and sugar?'

She turned sharply, blinking to clear her head as she saw Max was waiting to pour her coffee, the maid having already quietly departed. 'Black. Thank you,' she added stiffly.

What was she doing here? she asked herself once again. Had she secretly hoped? Had a part of her still thought that perhaps there had been some sort of mistake—

'Thank you.' She moved to take the cup out of his hand, her gaze not quite meeting his as he looked down at her probingly.

January, careful not to let their hands touch as she took the cup from him, moved away from him abruptly to once again look out of the window, blinking back the sudden tears that blurred her vision.

She had been so angry earlier, at the realization of exactly who he was, at what she believed to be his duplicity; now she just felt miserable. Because it was all over? Because for that brief forty-eight hours she had felt wrapped in Max's interest in her? Had known a feeling of being cared for that she hadn't felt since her father had died? Was that why she so desperately wanted to cry?

How stupid she was. She should have known, should

have guessed, that having a man like Max interested in her just couldn't be real. After all, what was she really but a part-time farmer and singer? Hardly the sort of woman Max could ever be serious about. For all she knew about him, he could already be a married man! The very thought of that was enough to stiffen her backbone.

'Max—'

'January—'

They both began talking at once, January giving Max a rueful grimace as she turned to face him. 'You first,' she invited huskily.

His expression was bleak, eyes icy blue, letting her know that whatever he was going to say, she wasn't going to like it.

Whatever he said now, Max knew January wasn't going to like it. If he mentioned Jude and renewed his offer to buy the farm, January wasn't going to like it. If he tried to explain—once again!—that he really hadn't known she was one of the Calendar sisters, he knew she wasn't going to like that, either. Or, indeed, believe him.

Besides, what was the point in even trying to convince her that he was telling the truth about that when he had already decided to back away from that particular situation himself? Back away—he was backpedalling so fast he was surprised she couldn't hear the pedals going round!

God, she was beautiful, he inwardly acknowledged achingly.

Yes, she was.

But now that he knew who she was, the closeness of her family, he also knew that whatever she might have said about love the night they'd first met, she was actually the sort of woman who wouldn't settle for anything less than marriage—and, no matter how attracted he was to her, the very thought of being married, to anyone, gave him an icy lump of panic in the pit of his stomach.

His mouth thinned grimly. 'I spoke to Jude Marshall earlier,' he bit out forcefully. 'He's willing to increase his offer.'

January recoiled as if he had actually struck her, and it took every ounce of Max's will-power not to take her in his arms, to tell her that everything would be okay, that while he was around no one would ever take the farm away from her, or anything else, if she didn't want them to.

But who was he kidding? He had known Jude most of his life, might be a trusted friend as well as employee, but he also knew the other man well enough to know that what Jude wanted, he got, usually by fair means, but if those means ultimately failed...! Jude had left him in absolutely no doubt earlier that he wanted the Calendar farm, and that he intended getting it.

Max's own inner feelings of a conflict of interest simply wouldn't come into the other man's equation!

Max thrust his hands into the pockets of his denims, his fists tightly clenched. 'My advice to you all is to seriously consider this second offer,' he told January harshly.

Her eyes widened indignantly as she snapped, 'I wasn't aware I had asked for your advice!'

He shrugged with seeming unconcern, hating himself for talking to her in this way, but at the same time knowing that he couldn't back down now from the stance he had taken. Couldn't? More like daredn't, he acknowledged self-disgustedly. Conflict of interest, be damned; he had made his choice in Jude's favour the moment he'd realized just how deeply involved he already was with January. Having her hate him for that choice was the price he had to pay.

'I'm offering it anyway,' he drawled dismissively. 'Jude isn't a man to take no for an answer.'

Her eyes flashed deeply grey. 'Then the two of you must have a lot in common.'

She meant to be insulting, and she succeeded. Although there was no denying, Max accepted hardly, that she unwittingly told the truth. The two men were similar in lots of ways, both successful at what they did, both still bachelors at thirty-seven, and both intending to stay that way.

If not for the same reasons.

Jude made no secret of the fact that although women fascinated him, they as quickly bored him in a one-to-one relationship, claimed that if he ever met the woman who didn't bore him after a few days' acquaintance he would marry her. Whereas Max had no intention of marrying ever, for any reason, least of all love.

He had looked at January on New Year's Eve, and known he wanted her. But it was nothing more than that, he told himself determinedly. He wouldn't allow it to be.

Women, he had learnt at a very young age, were fickle creatures at best, took a man's love and used it as a weapon against him.

His expression was bleak now. 'Resorting to insults isn't going to help resolve this situation,' he rasped.

'Maybe not,' she accepted heavily. 'But it certainly makes me feel better!'

He gave a rueful shrug. 'Then feel free.'

She gave him a searching look. 'Max, can I ask you a question?'

He stiffened warily, not liking the look in her eyes now. 'Go ahead,' he invited tensely.

'How do you sleep at night?' she scorned.

The last two nights—very badly. Usually—very well. But he knew that wasn't what she was really asking!

His mouth twisted derisively. 'January, whatever you may or may not think of me personally, Jude's offer is a fair one—'

'I'm not interested in anything to do with Jude Marshall!' she burst out scathingly. 'Until recently, I had never even heard of the man—and I wish I still hadn't!' she added disgustedly. 'I'm more interested in knowing how you can bear to be used as his—as his—'

'Careful, January,' Max warned softly. 'In view of your obvious anger, there are some insults I'm willing to accept—others I am not,' he added hardly. 'I'm a lawyer. I have never been guilty of committing any sort of unlawful act.'

'Not unlawful, maybe,' she allowed heatedly. 'But there is such a thing as a moral wrong.'

'Granted,' he acknowledged icily. 'But as far as the Calendar family is concerned, I can't see where I have been guilty of that either!'

'You—you can't see—!' January stared at him incredulously. 'You don't consider deliberately setting out to seduce one of us, in order to divide and conquer, to be morally wrong?'

His eyes narrowed coldly. 'You're referring to yourself?'

'Of course I'm referring to myself!' she confirmed

impatiently, becoming suddenly still as she looked at him suspiciously. 'Unless—'

'Don't even suggest it, January,' he warned softly. 'So far I believe I have remained calm and reasonable during your diatribe of accusations—but if you proceed with the present one I may not be answerable for the consequences!'

'*You* may not be—'

'January, I don't believe this conversation is doing anything to calm this situation down,' he cut in impatiently, not sure how much longer he could stand here and take her insults without pulling her into his arms and kissing her into silence!

Which, in the circumstances, wouldn't calm the situation down either!

His mouth twisted. 'Our previous—friendship, may have given you the impression that you had the freedom to come here and throw wild accusations at me.' He scowled darkly. 'But I happen to think otherwise—'

'Friendship?' she echoed furiously. 'Friendship!' she repeated disgustedly, shaking her head. 'We were never friends, Max, and you know it—' She was suddenly silenced as Max's mouth came down forcefully on hers.

He hadn't been able to stop himself. Could no longer stand here and have January look at him with such dislike and loathing. Not that he thought kissing her was going to make her dislike him any less—he really just couldn't help himself!

He might never know a moment's peace again, might never again have complete possession of his soul, either, he realized dazedly. But for the moment, kissing January, holding her close against him, touching the silkiness of her skin, was all that mattered.

CHAPTER SIX

SHE should stop this.

Now.

Yet January couldn't bring herself to do that, inwardly knew that this might never happen again, that she might never again know the taste and feel of Max's lips on hers, the caress of his hands against the warmth of her burning skin.

And she wanted those things.

Wanted them so badly.

Wanted Max.

His hair was like silk against her hands as her fingers became entwined in its darkness, deepening their kiss, heat and moisture, a duel of tongues that spoke of their desire for each other.

January made no demur as her coat fell to the carpeted floor, at the warmth of Max's hands beneath the thickness of her zipped top, flesh catching fire at the caress of his hands against the dampness of her skin.

She was aware once again of that oneness, of not knowing where she ended and Max began, every particle of her seeming joined to him, two halves of a perfect whole.

She groaned low in her throat as he broke the kiss, that groan turning to a throaty ache as his lips moved slowly across her cheek, down the sensitive column of her neck, to the pulsing hollow at its base, lips and tongue probing moistly there, pulses of pleasure shooting down the length of her spine to ignite a hitherto unknown warmth between trembling thighs.

The zip of her top moved slowly down beneath Max's searching fingers, he bending his head as his lips followed the same path, January's back arching instinctively as she felt the moisture of his mouth through the silky material of her bra, his tongue moving in a slow caress over the pouting invitation of her nipple.

His hands encircled the slenderness of her bared waist now, holding her against the hardness of his thighs as his lips paid homage to the warm swell of her breasts. And lower.

January moved against him invitingly, her fingers once again entangled in the darkness of his hair, holding him against her, never wanting this pleasure to stop.

And it didn't, not when Max bent to lift her up in his arms, or when he carried her through to the bedroom to lay her down on top of the bed, or when he lay his long length beside her, his mouth once again taking fierce possession of hers.

Despite the difference in their heights, their bodies seemed to curve perfectly together as they lay turned into each other's arms, January's hands free to touch him in return now, caressing the hardness of his muscled back as they pressed closely together.

She gasped at the unfamiliar touch of hands against the bareness of her thighs, able to feel Max's warmth through the lacy material of her panties, that gasp turning to a groan of pleasure as he easily sought and found the centre of her pleasure, the whole of her body feeling like molten lava now.

'January, if you want me to stop, then you have to say so now—before it's too late!'

She gasped at the sound of Max's voice, felt as if a

bucket of ice cold water had just been thrown over her, as if the roof above them had disappeared to allow the cold snow to fall on her burning skin, awakening her from— From what?

She fell back on the bed, staring up at Max with darkly haunted eyes, his own eyes still dark with desire as he looked at her searchingly.

'Don't look at me like that!' he finally groaned harshly.

She breathed shallowly, her tongue moving to moisten suddenly dry lips. 'Like what?'

Was that husky rasp really her voice? It had sounded completely unlike her usual confident tones, like the voice of a stranger.

And perhaps that was what she had become, even to herself. Because she knew only too well that if Max hadn't spoken and broken the spell it would no longer have just seemed as if they were two halves of a whole—it would have been a reality!

Max continued to look down at her frowningly for several long, searching seconds before flinging himself back on the pillow to stare up at the ceiling. 'As if I'm some sort of monster you need protecting from!' he rasped coldly.

Had she really looked at him in that way? If she had, then it was totally unfair—because the only person she needed protecting from was herself!

'Max—'

He swung away from her as she would have reached out and touched his arm, swinging his legs down to sit up on the side of the bed. 'I think you had better leave, January,' he muttered grimly. 'Before either of us does or says something we're going to regret!'

Hadn't they already done that?

January knew that she certainly had. And one glance at Max's grimly set features told her that he wasn't in the least happy about what had happened, either!

She sat up, fumbling with the zip on her jeans, pulling the sides of her sweater together, her fingers shaking now as she tried to put the zipper together. This was so— Why wouldn't this thing—?

'Here—let me,' Max bit out tautly, at the same time reaching out—with hands that were completely steady, January noticed self-derisively—to put the zipper together and pull up the silver catch.

January looked at him beneath lowered lashes, looking, searching desperately, for some sign of the man from seconds ago, the man who had trembled with the same desire she had. All she could see was Max Golding, his hair slightly ruffled perhaps, a nerve pulsing—with anger or suppressed desire?—in the hardness of his cheek, but otherwise he looked just as self-assured as ever!

'Your look of reproach is a little late in coming, don't you think?' he drawled dryly. 'As well as being misdirected!' he added scathingly.

January flinched as if he had hit her, his words certainly wounding, if not physically then emotionally.

'I have to go.' She pushed back the tangle of her hair as she scrambled over to the side of the bed, wondering when she had ever felt so miserable. Never, came the unequivocal answer!

'Running away, January?' Max murmured tauntingly as she reached the bedroom door.

She turned to give him a sharp reply, the words catching in her throat as she saw herself reflected in the mirror across the room, seeing herself as she never had before.

Her hair was a tangled cloud about her shoulders, her eyes a wild dark grey, her face a white blur, her lips bruised red with passion. She looked exactly what she was—a woman who had recently been roused to a passion she might never recover from!

She swallowed hard, forcing her gaze from that wanton reflection as she looked across at Max contemptuously. 'Not running, Max, walking,' she corrected with hard derision. 'I should never have come here in the first place!' she added bitterly.

'No, you shouldn't,' he acknowledged hardly, moving to sit back on the bed, one arm behind his head as he rested back against the headboard. 'A short time ago, you asked me how I sleep at night,' he reminded tauntingly. 'Well, I can tell you, the answer to that is "very rarely alone",' he drawled mockingly, blue eyes openly laughing at her now.

January stiffened defensively at the pain his words caused, easily able to envisage him in bed with a sea of faceless women—especially with him sprawled out on the bed in that telling way!

Her mouth twisted disgustedly. 'Well, it looks as if you lucked out tonight, doesn't it?' she scorned.

He gave a lazy glance at the gold watch nestling amongst the dark hairs on his wrist. 'There's still time.' He shrugged.

January gasped, glaring at him now as she spat out the words, 'You're despicable!'

He gave another shrug, blue eyes as hard as sapphires now. 'Go home, January,' he scorned dismissively. 'Come back when you've grown up a little.'

Her hands were clenched so tightly at her sides she could feel her fingernails digging into her palms. 'It really was all an act from start to finish, wasn't it?' she burst out emotionally. 'That remark about love at first sight was part of your seduction, too,' she added chokingly.

He grimaced. 'Most women, I've found, respond to the word love rather than lust.' He gave a humourless smile. 'I have to admit, January, you shocked the hell out of me when you called it exactly what it is!' He gave an appreciative inclination of his head.

She felt sick, mostly at herself, she admitted; she had guessed what sort of man Max was from the beginning, had no excuse for what had just happened between them.

'But the feeling of lust, thank goodness, isn't confined to one person,' Max continued dismissively. 'Besides, January—' his gaze was once again mocking '—I have a feeling that if either of us isn't going to sleep tonight it's going to be you!' He looked across at her challengingly.

She had to get out of here. Away from Max. Away from this room, and the memory of how close they had come to making love…!

'My conscience is clear, Max—how about yours?' she scorned, head held high.

He grimaced dismissively. 'The same.'

She gave a disgusted shake of her head. 'Then you must have a very different idea of what I consider acceptable behaviour!'

He shrugged. 'For someone who was leaving at least five minutes ago, you don't seem in any particular hurry to do so?' He quirked mocking brows.

January drew in a sharp breath at his taunt. 'Don't worry, Max—I'm going. And I never want to see you again!' She breathed agitatedly.

He gave a grim smile. 'No chance of that happening,

I'm afraid, January,' he drawled. 'After all, I'm still negotiating on behalf of the Marshall Corporation to buy your family farm.'

'Over my dead body!' she told him with feeling.

'If you insist on driving in snowstorms—that might very well be the case,' he mocked dryly.

She had to go. Now. Before she totally humiliated herself and began to cry!

'Take care, January,' Max murmured softly. 'I hope you sleep well,' he added tauntingly.

She gave a pained frown at this last comment, turning sharply on her heel and almost running from the room, only lingering long enough to grab her coat from the floor where it had fallen before hurrying from the hotel suite as if the devil himself were at her heels.

He was hateful. Horrible. The most horrible man she had ever met in her life!

How could she have been so stupid?

How could she have so totally misjudged a person?

How—?

'January…?'

She looked up frowningly as she crossed the reception area of the hotel, her brow clearing slightly as she recognized John, the barman, obviously just coming in for his evening shift.

He looked at her concernedly. 'Hey, are you okay?'

Okay? She might never be 'okay' again!

'Fine,' she assured him huskily, hoping she didn't look as bad as she felt.

She had straightened her hair a little while travelling down in the lift, but she hadn't been able to do anything about the paleness of her face, or that slightly bruised look to her lips.

'You don't look okay.' Obviously John wasn't fooled for a minute, still frowning his concern. 'Come through to the bar and have a brandy,' he encouraged worriedly.

She gave a humourless laugh, shaking her head. 'I won't, if you don't mind. I've already had one accident today,' she explained ruefully. 'My sister will kill me if I prang her car, too!'

His eyes widened. 'You've been involved in an accident?'

'Only with a ditch.' She grimaced. 'I really do have to go, John,' she apologized lightly. 'Is it still snowing?' She really had no idea how long she had been in Max's hotel suite, or what the weather was like, either!

'No, it's stopped,' John told her distractedly. 'You really don't look well, January, are you sure you wouldn't like me to get someone to take over in the bar for me for a couple of hours and drive you home?'

'That's very kind of you.' She touched his arm gratefully. 'But no,' she insisted. 'I drove here, I can drive back.'

'Meridew didn't call you in, did he?' John muttered disgustedly.

'No, nothing like that.' She avoided his concerned gaze. 'I really do have to go, John,' she told him briskly. 'Have a good evening!' She hurried away before he could delay her further.

Or question her further! The fewer people who knew she had been stupid enough to visit Max in his hotel suite, the better!

It was bad enough that she knew. That she was totally aware of what an idiot she had been. Of how totally she had misjudged Max's true nature.

Well, she wouldn't make that mistake again. In fact, she meant it when she said she hoped she never saw him again!

Good, Max. Very good, he congratulated himself as he still lay back on the bed. He had deliberately set out to make January dislike him—and he had succeeded!

Only too well.

The look of loathing she had given him before leaving told him that she didn't just dislike him, she hated him.

Well, it was what he wanted, wasn't it?

Of course it was.

He had deliberately set out to break those tenuous emotional ties with her, to make sure that there was no further conflict of interest. Now that he knew January was one of the Calendar sisters, and Jude refused to give up on buying the Calendar farm, it had been the only thing he could have done.

Then why did he feel so miserable at having succeeded in what he set out to do? Because he did feel miserable. More miserable than he had felt in his life before. Ever. And that included having his mother walk out on his father and him when he was only five years old.

He wasn't naïve, knew that early experience had tempered his future relationships with women, his decision never to fall in love, never to trust any woman enough to lay himself open to that vulnerability.

But in all honesty he couldn't even remember what his mother looked like any more. It was only the devastating loneliness of her desertion that stayed with him. Always.

Well, he certainly had nothing further to worry about in that way where January was concerned; she had really meant it when she said she never wanted to see him again.

Why did that hurt so much?

Because it wasn't lust he felt for January at all, because he—

He had to get out of here, Max decided, standing up compulsively; even he couldn't stand his own company at this particular moment! He needed to do something, go somewhere, anything to distract his thoughts from January and the way he had deliberately hurt her.

It was almost nine o'clock, he discovered when he got downstairs, but even so John was alone in the bar when Max walked into the room. Which suited his mood perfectly; the last thing he felt in the mood for at the moment was a lot of chattering people around him having fun!

'A large whisky,' he requested as he sat down on one of the bar stools.

'Lousy weather, isn't it?' John placed the drink on the bar in front of Max.

'Looks as if you'll have a quiet evening.' Max nodded grimly, taking a large gulp of the fiery alcohol. 'Don't you ever have an evening off?' he prompted abruptly; he might not feel like having chattering people around him, but his own exclusive company wasn't what he wanted at the moment either!

John grinned. 'Mondays and Tuesdays.'

Max grimaced. 'That must play havoc with your social life?'

'What social life?' John dismissed pointedly. 'Still, it's a job, which is more than a lot of people have.' He shrugged. 'You missed January, earlier, by the way,' he added lightly as he moved along the bar filling up the bowls of nuts.

Max stiffened just at the sound of her name. So much for getting out of his hotel room, of doing something to keep thoughts of January at bay!

'She seemed…upset,' John added frowningly.

'Did she?' Max kept his tone bland, not wanting to get into any sort of conversation about January. Certainly not the reason she had seemed upset!

John's brow cleared. 'Perhaps—'

'Mr Golding?'

Max had been so intent on his conversation with the barman, so deliberately trying not to think of January 'upset', that he had been completely unaware of the fact that he and John were no longer alone in the bar.

But there was no mistaking the sound of that voice. No mistaking its likeness to January's. Except he knew, after the way they had parted earlier, that it certainly wasn't January.

He turned slowly to find May Calendar standing behind him, keeping his expression neutral as he stood up. 'Miss Calendar.' He nodded politely.

It was a couple of hours since January had left the hotel, which meant the two sisters could have spoken when she'd returned home. Or not. Until he knew the answer to that, Max intended remaining detached. If wary.

Irritation flickered briefly in those deep green eyes as May looked at their surroundings. 'Could we possibly go somewhere and talk?' she requested abruptly.

'Certainly,' Max acquiesced evenly. 'How about that table over there?' He pointed to the far side of the room. 'Perhaps John could get you a drink—?'

'I would rather go somewhere a little more—private,' May briskly interrupted him. 'No offence.' She gave John an apologetic grimace.

'None taken,' the barman assured her happily. 'I wouldn't be in here either if I didn't work here!'

May gave an obliging laugh before once again making Max the focal point of that steady deep green gaze. 'Mr Golding?' she prompted pointedly.

He still had no idea whether May had spoken to January on her return earlier, or even if January would have confided in her eldest sister what had happened if they had spoken. But perhaps it would be better to err on the side of caution; if May intended hitting him, it would probably be better if it wasn't done in a public place!

'Let's go upstairs to my suite,' he suggested briskly, signing for his drink before escorting the eldest Calendar sister from the bar.

It was uncanny how physically alike the three sisters were, Max ruefully acknowledged, although he already knew from his two visits to the farm that May, as the eldest sister, was a force to be reckoned with, that she didn't suffer fools gladly. More importantly, she wasn't impressed by him in any way, shape or form!

Well, at the moment, after the way he had treated January earlier, he couldn't say he was too impressed by himself either!

'I believe one of the quieter lounges will do as well for my purpose,' May informed him dryly as she paused in the reception area.

Perhaps she wasn't going to hit him, after all…

She obviously had no intention of being alone with him in his hotel suite, either!

'Fine.' He gave an acknowledging inclination of his head. 'There are some small conference rooms down this corridor.' He indicated that May should precede him. 'I'm sure the management won't mind if we use one for a few minutes.'

Almost as beautiful as her sister—in his eyes January was still the most beautiful woman he had ever seen!—May also had a determined tilt to her chin, a way of looking at him with those emerald-coloured eyes, as if she could see straight through him. Which wasn't a very comfortable feeling, Max acknowledged with an inner squirm!

'Fine,' May finally agreed slowly, leading the way down the corridor.

This was the first time Max had seen the eldest Calendar sister out of the bulky sweaters and faded denims she wore to work in on the farm; she was stunning in the black jacket, thin emerald-coloured jumper and pencil-slim skirt, her legs as long and shapely as January's in the heeled shoes.

Why the hell weren't any of these women already married? Max wondered incredulously; it would have solved so much of the problem if they had been! Were all the single men in the area blind? Or was it the sisters who just weren't interested?

May entered the conference room to turn and look at him, her mouth twisting derisively as she saw the way Max was watching her—almost as if she were able to read his thoughts. And found them amusing.

'Many men have tried, and many men have failed!' she drawled mockingly, an imp of mischief leaping now in the beauty of her eyes.

'Why have they failed?' Max didn't even make a pretence of not understanding what she was talking about.

She shrugged. 'Maybe they didn't try hard enough.'

After the way he had deliberately alienated January

earlier, this was not, Max told himself firmly, the sort of conversation he should be having with any of the Calendar sisters! 'What can I do for you, Miss Calendar?' he prompted hardly.

The mischief faded from her eyes, leaving them as cold and hard as the jewels they resembled. 'Stay away from my sister,' she told him flatly. 'And please don't pretend not to know which sister I'm talking about,' she added as he would have spoken.

'I wasn't going to,' he assured her bleakly. 'But, unless I'm mistaken, after this evening January will never come near me, through choice, ever again!' Hadn't she said as much?

May looked at him with narrowed eyes for several long minutes. 'What makes you say that?' she finally murmured slowly.

'That isn't for me to say,' he bit out tautly; was it possible the sisters hadn't already spoken this evening, that May was here on some crusade of her own that had nothing to do with what had happened between January and himself earlier...?

May's mouth twisted humourlessly. 'Isn't it a little late in the day for you to be acting gentlemanly?'

He stiffened at the deliberate insult. 'You know, Miss Calendar, I believe I've already taken quite enough insults from your family for one day!' he rasped.

That impish humour flickered once again in the depths of her green eyes. 'That's good.' She nodded unrepentantly. 'But, unless I'm mistaken, March hasn't even started yet!'

Max gave a heavy sigh. 'Tell her not to bother,' he muttered tautly. 'You know...' he sat on the side of the long conference table '...I came here thinking this was just going to be another routine job, the usual buying and exchanging of contracts—no one warned me I was going to have to deal with the Calendar Mob!' He shook his head self-disgustedly.

May gave a throaty chuckle. 'We try to keep that one quiet!'

'Your secret is out,' Max informed her dryly. 'And for some reason my employer, Jude Marshall, thinks you're three little old ladies who sit and knit bedsocks in front of the fire on cold winter evenings!' He shook his head derisively.

'Really?' May said interestedly. 'Perhaps Mr Marshall should come here and do his own dirty work,' she suggested grimly.

'Perhaps he should.' Max nodded; the same idea had occurred to him during the last few hours!

'In the meantime—' May's gaze had became suddenly intent '—don't hurt my sister, Mr Golding,' she told him softly. 'January has already been hurt enough, without adding you to the list!'

Max looked at her sharply. 'What do you mean?' Had there already been someone in January's life, some man, who had let her down and hurt her? Somehow the thought of that did not please him one little bit!

'Never mind.' May gave an enigmatic shake of her head. 'Unless your intentions are serious— Are they?' She looked at him with narrowed eyes.

His mouth tightened. 'No,' he bit out harshly.

'As I thought.' She gave an acknowledging inclination of her head, picking up her bag in preparation of leaving. 'Then my advice to you is to leave January alone.'

'And if I don't?' he challenged warily.

May shrugged. 'Then the Calendar Mob will have to pay you another visit!'

Max couldn't help it, he smiled. 'I wish I had had a sister like you to look out for me when I was younger!' Instead he had been an only child, brought up alone by his father, a man who had also never trusted in love again.

But who, by that single act, had died alone, too…?

May gave him a rueful grimace. 'Somehow, Max, I doubt you've ever let anyone do that,' she murmured enigmatically. 'Now, if you will excuse me? I've said all I came here to say.' She walked over to the door, quietly letting herself out.

Now exactly what had she meant by that last remark? Max wondered frowningly. Had May guessed at the barrier he kept firmly around his heart? If so, how had she guessed?

Not that it particularly mattered; her message concerning January had come across loud and clear.

Well, May Calendar needn't worry herself on his account; he had no intention of ever putting himself in a position of being close to January again. She was a definite no-no as far as he was concerned.

Except he couldn't stop himself wondering about the implication May had given of some man having hurt January in the recent past…

CHAPTER SEVEN

'WHAT do you want?' January gasped, having opened the farmhouse door to find Max standing on the doorstep beside her muddy boots.

It was barely thirty-six hours since she had last seen this man, the memory of Sunday evening not even having begun to fade from her mind—in fact, she doubted it ever would. Although she was certainly going to try to erase it!

She certainly didn't welcome the fact that Max had turned up at the farm when she was alone, March out at work, May having an appointment in town.

'I asked what you want,' she repeated hardly as Max made no effort to answer her, just standing on the doorstep staring at her, his face grim, a guarded look in those deep blue eyes.

'Are you okay?' he finally murmured harshly.

January gave him a scathing look. 'Why shouldn't I be okay?' she scorned derisively.

Surely he didn't think she would still be visibly upset about Sunday evening? If he did, he was going to be sadly disappointed! She had made a mistake, had totally humiliated herself as far as she was concerned, but there was no way she was going to let anyone see that. Certainly not Max. She had more pride than that.

Max thrust his hands into his denims pockets, the grimness of his expression not having eased in the slightest. 'It was on the television, on the local news, that there was another attack late last night,' he bit out tautly.

Her eyes widened. She hadn't heard anything about that. But then, she didn't have time to watch television in the day, and it was too early for March to have returned from work with any local gossip.

'And?' she prompted hardly.

He swallowed hard, grimacing. 'They are being particularly cagey about this one, not giving out any names, or other details, just that the latest victim had been badly beaten but was recovering in hospital.'

January glared her impatience. 'And?' Really, why didn't he just say what he had come here to say—and then leave? 'I'm really sorry there's been another attack, hope that the woman will be okay, but if you've come here to discuss buying the farm—'

'I haven't come here for that!' he cut in harshly, a nerve pulsing in his tightly clenched jaw.

She gave a puzzled shake of her head. 'Then why are you here?'

'Isn't it obvious?' he snapped frustratedly.

Not to her, no. He had made it clear on Sunday evening—painfully clear, she recalled with an inner wince—that other than wanting to buy the farm he had no personal interest in her than as a possible casual bed-partner. A role she had made clear was completely unacceptable to her.

'I'm afraid not.' She gave a puzzled shake of her head.

Max gave a sigh of impatience. 'Haven't you been listening to a word I said?'

She gave a humourless smile. 'When usually most people hang on your every word?'

He scowled darkly. 'January, I'm more than aware of your opinion of me—'

'I doubt that very much!' she scorned; he couldn't possibly know how angry she still was. With him. But more so with herself.

She had been so careful after the mistake she had made the previous year, been friendly but distant to any man who might have shown an interest in her, hadn't even been out on a date since Ben had let her down so badly—only to end up making a complete idiot of herself over a man who was ten times more dangerous—to her heart!—than Ben had ever been!

Max gave the ghost of a smile. 'Oh, I think I am. But I heard that radio announcement and I— Where are March and May?'

'March is at work and May is at the dentist,' she dismissed.

He nodded grimly at this explanation for her sisters' absence.

'Obviously I made a mistake,' he dismissed hardly, preparing to leave.

January looked at him frowningly as he began to walk back to his car. He was arrogant. Hateful. Had hurt her pretty badly on Sunday evening. But the things he had said just now… Could he possibly—? Had he come here because—?

'Would you like to come in for a cup of coffee?' she heard herself offer abruptly.

Max turned slowly back to look at her, his expression once again wary. 'In the circumstances, that's very kind of you,' he finally murmured slowly.

She gave a shrug. 'Didn't you know—? I'm a kind person!' she attempted to dismiss lightly.

Whereas, in reality, she had no idea why she had

offered him a cup of coffee. It certainly wasn't because she wanted to spend any time in his company; she usually came off worst in any encounter the two of them had, verbal or otherwise!

Then why had she made the offer? Perhaps because she suspected, from the things Max had said, that he had come here because he had thought it was either her, or one of her sisters, who had been attacked the previous night. And if that were the case...

'The offer is only open for another ten seconds, Max,' she told him derisively. 'My toes are starting to freeze standing here!' she added with a rueful glance down at her feet.

Max looked down, too, the frown clearing from his brow. 'You really were serious about the bare feet, weren't you?' he murmured incredulously as he followed her into the kitchen, closing the door—and the extreme cold—behind him.

January glanced back from placing the kettle on the Aga. 'I don't tell lies, either, Max,' she told him huskily.

And then wished she hadn't. Whether her suspicion as to why he had come here was correct or not, she would rather not think of any of their previous conversations. Or anything else!

'If you must know, my feet are bare because I was just on my way to my bedroom for a pair of dry socks when you knocked on the door; I was coming back from the barn when I slipped and fell into a snowdrift. The snow went in my boots,' she explained abruptly.

Max raised dark brows. 'Are you always this accident prone? First a ditch and now a snowdrift,' he added mockingly.

'Hmm.' She grimaced. 'I do seem to have bumped

into more than my fair share of immovable objects just recently, don't I?' she dismissed self-derisively.

Max being the prime one!

Something that he seemed all too aware of as his mouth tightened. 'January—'

'Sit down, Max,' she invited with a general wave in the direction of the kitchen table and chairs. 'Coffee is almost ready.' She turned back to the task in hand, deliberately keeping herself busy for the next few minutes, although she was very aware of Max as he sat at the table watching her every move.

Why had he come here today? Was it really, as she suspected, because he had been concerned that one of the sisters might have been the Night Striker's latest victim? But if that were the reason, wouldn't that have to mean that he actually cared—?

'Did May tell you that she came to see me on Sunday evening?'

'Yes, she told me,' January confirmed lightly, picking up the two mugs of coffee before strolling over to place one of them in front of Max and sitting down opposite him. 'Help yourself to sugar.' She indicated the bowl that stood in the middle of the table. 'Since our mother died, May has been the family champion, I'm afraid.' The lightness of her tone totally belied the fact that she had been furious with May when she'd returned on Sunday evening and admitted where she had been.

Max gave a humourless smile. 'She certainly did a good job of warning me off you!'

'A little too late, obviously.' She nodded, staring down at her steaming mug of coffee.

May had been protecting March and January for as long as the two of them could remember, the two younger sisters, as they'd got older, often finding this fierce protectiveness irksome to say the least. January had been so furious at May's uninvited intervention on her behalf on Sunday evening that the two sisters had only just started speaking to each other again.

Although, to give Max his due, he obviously hadn't told her sister what had happened between the two of them a couple of hours before May's arrival at the hotel.

'When did your mother die?' Max prompted huskily.

January looked up. 'I was three, so…twenty-two years ago now,' she acknowledged with a pained frown.

Max frowned darkly. 'That must have been—' He shook his head. 'I was five when my mother left,' he said abruptly.

And as instantly regretted the admission, January could see by the surprise in his eyes he wasn't quick enough to hide, his expression becoming guarded. Making January wonder if he had ever confided that to anyone before today. Max certainly didn't come across as a man who was comfortable confiding his personal life to other people.

'Shouldn't you go and put something on your feet?' he prompted with unwarranted harshness.

'Yes, I should,' January acknowledged lightly, standing up. 'I won't be long,' she told him as she left the room.

But long enough to give him chance to put his defences back in order; the last thing she needed was to feel any sort of empathy with Max Golding—worse, to actually feel sorry for him!

He wouldn't welcome the emotion anyway. Any

more than he would welcome having her in love with him.

Which, she now realised, despite all those hateful things he had said to her on Sunday evening, she most certainly was.

May, it seemed, had given her warning of caution to the wrong person!

What was he doing here? Max questioned himself impatiently as January left the kitchen. He had known as soon as January had opened the door to his knock that she wasn't the woman who had been attacked last night, so why hadn't he just made his excuses and left?

Because he couldn't! Because he had had one hell of a scare this morning when he'd heard that television announcement about the attacker's latest victim being in hospital! Because just seeing January standing on the doorstep, so obviously alive and well, meant he hadn't been able to drag himself away from just looking at her!

Although why on earth he had compounded that by telling her about his mother, he had no idea!

He never talked about his mother's desertion. Never told anyone of the effect it had had on him. It simply wasn't good enough to claim he had merely been returning January's confidence about her own mother. Her mother had died, for goodness' sake, not walked out on her!

He had to get away from here. Had to go. Now!

But before he could even stand up to leave the outside door opened and May walked in, her eyes widening in surprise as she saw him sitting comfortably ensconced at the kitchen table. Although she recovered well, he thought, that obvious look of surprise turning into a polite smile of enquiry.

'January is upstairs putting on dry socks,' he told her dryly.

Dark brows rose over mocking green eyes. 'What did she do with the last pair?' May drawled, taking off her jacket to hang it on the back of the kitchen door.

'Fell in a snowdrift,' Max supplied wryly.

'Ah,' May nodded, obviously not in the least surprised by the explanation. 'Can I get you another cup of coffee, or are you okay?' she offered as she boiled up some water for her own hot drink.

'I'm fine, thanks,' Max dismissed. 'How did your check-up go?'

May turned to him with a puzzled frown. 'Sorry?'

'January said you were at the dentist,' he explained.

'Ah.' May nodded. 'It was fine,' she added dismissively, busying herself making her cup of coffee.

Max's gaze narrowed shrewdly as he continued to watch her. He hadn't missed May's complete puzzlement at his mention of a check-up, or the fact that her gaze hadn't quite met his when she'd answered him; if May Calendar had been to the dentist then his name wasn't Maxim Patrick Golding!

Which begged the question, where had May really been? And why had she lied to January about it?

Not that it was really any of his business, but—

'May!' January greeted more than a little self-consciously as she came back into the kitchen and found her sister there. 'How did—?'

'We've already done the dentist bit,' Max cut in derisively. 'Your sister's teeth are as healthy as yours,' he added huskily, knowing as he saw January's confused blush that his barb had hit home, that she remembered as well as he did the nip she had given him on the shoulder on Sunday evening with those healthy teeth, as he'd kissed and caressed her breasts.

What January couldn't know was that he still had a bruise on his shoulder as proof of those healthy teeth!

The blush deepened in January's cheeks even as she shot him a warning look.

Ah, so the protective May still didn't know what had happened between January and himself on Sunday evening!

Not that he was exactly proud of himself for the way things had got so out of hand that evening. Or the way he had deliberately made light of it to January afterwards…!

Because, no matter what he might have said to her, he hadn't slept at all on Sunday night. Last night either, for that matter. Instead he had lain awake both those nights arguing with himself. Half of him had wanted to tell January that he hadn't meant any of the hurtful things he had said to her, that it had been pure defence on his part. But the other half of him knew that he would be admitting so much more than that if he were to tell her those things. And that he simply couldn't—wouldn't!—do.

The television announcement this morning about yet another attack had been his undoing, though; the thought that it might be January lying in that hospital bed, battered and bruised, had been enough to throw him into a panic.

Not that coming to the farm had been his first instinct. No, he had telephoned the police first, who had refused to give out any information whatsoever about the attack, least of all the victim's name. The hospital had been no more forthcoming, either. Leaving him no choice—unless he wanted to just sit and go quietly out of his mind with worry!—but to come to the farm.

But now that he was here, could see for himself that January was unharmed, he really had no idea what he was still doing here.

Or how to make a dignified exit!

'I should be going—'

'Don't feel you have to leave on my account,' May drawled as she leant back against the Aga, coffee mug in her hand as she looked across at him with mocking green eyes.

His mouth tightened. 'I'm sure I've kept you both from your work enough for one day,' he insisted hardly.

'It can wait.' May shrugged. 'No matter how hard or how long you work on a farm, Max, there's always more to be done,' she added ruefully.

He frowned. 'In that case—'

'That doesn't mean we're interested in selling it,' January told him harshly.

Max looked across at her calmly. 'I was actually going to say, why don't you get someone in to help you if there's so much to do?'

'Good question,' May derided.

'It isn't good at all!' January corrected snappily. 'There's the little problem of paying someone to help.' She turned on Max sharply. 'Something, it must be obvious even to you, that we aren't in a position to do.'

'January…' May rebuked softly. 'Max was only asking,' she reasoned gently before turning to give Max a rueful smile. 'We did have some help last year after—after our father died,' she explained huskily. 'It didn't work out.' She shrugged.

He couldn't help noticing that January looked rather

pale now, May's gaze once again evasive, making him wonder in what way it hadn't worked out.

He shrugged. 'It was just a thought.'

'A totally impractical one,' January snapped scornfully. 'Although that must be rather good for you to hear,' she continued scathingly. 'After all, it would suit your plans perfectly if we were forced into selling the farm because we simply couldn't manage it any more!'

'January—'

'Don't be fooled by him for a minute, May,' January harshly interrupted her sister's reasoning tone. 'Max—and the Marshall Corporation—would like nothing better than for us to fall flat on our faces! Well, dream on, Max!' she told him forcefully. 'You will never get your mercenary hands on our farm! Now, if you'll excuse me,' she added hardly, grabbing her coat from the back of one of the chairs. 'You can stay and talk to him if you want to, May, but I have work to do!'

The room seemed to reverberate as she slammed the door behind her, May's wince matching Max's as he glanced across at her ruefully.

'What did you do to upset her this time?' May mused with a grimace.

'Do I need to "do" anything in order to upset January?' he came back wryly.

'Probably not,' May sighed.

'That's what I thought.' He nodded, his gaze narrowing. 'What was his name?' he rasped.

May looked at him undecidedly for several long seconds, and then she gave a rueful shrug. 'Ben,' she supplied economically.

His admiration for this woman seemed to grow by the minute. She had obviously taken over the role of mother to her two younger sisters while only aged five or six, still a baby herself, in fact, was possessed of a lively intelligence, and her beauty was of the inner as well as outer kind.

'Thank you.' He gave an acknowledging inclination of his head.

May frowned. 'For what?'

'For not insulting my intelligence by denying there was a "he",' Max drawled. 'That "he" was the hired help you had here last summer. I'm also guessing it's the same "he" who hurt January. The same "he" who prompted your warning me off her on Sunday evening,' he added ruefully.

'What would be the point in my denying any of that?' May shrugged. 'I realized on Sunday evening that I had probably said more than I should have done.' She sighed self-disgustedly. 'You're an intelligent man—'

'Thank you again,' he drawled dryly.

'That doesn't mean I like you!' she snapped, green eyes flashing a warning.

'That's a pity…' he smiled ruefully '…because I like you,' he explained at her questioning glance. 'Oh, not in that way,' he assured her as her glance became sceptical. 'One Calendar sister, I've discovered, is one too many!'

'I'm glad about that,' May drawled. 'Max, what are you doing with my little sister?'

He sighed, that sigh quickly becoming a grimace. 'How the hell should I know?' he murmured heavily.

She laughed incredulously. 'Well, if you don't know I certainly don't!'

What *was* he doing? January had made it more than clear when they'd parted on Sunday that she never intended seeing him again through choice, and he knew her well enough to believe she meant it.

So instead the mountain had come to Mohammed. Because he had feared for January's safety after hearing about the latest attack.

But he could have picked up the telephone, called the farm, then any one of the sisters could have given him that information.

Instead he had chosen to drive out here in order to see for himself that January was safe and well.

Why?

'Have you worked it out yet, Max?'

He looked sharply across at May, her too-innocent expression belied by the laughter gleaming in those intelligent green eyes.

'Tell you what,' she continued lightly. 'Go back to your hotel for a few hours, give January chance to calm down,' she added wryly. 'And then come back here this evening and have dinner with us.'

Max's gaze narrowed on her suspiciously. Why was May inviting him to dinner? She had no more reason to trust him than did her sisters…

May laughed softly at his obvious confusion. 'Mark it down as a thank-you for preventing me from telling another lie earlier—when January was about to ask me about my dental appointment,' she told him huskily.

So he had been right about that. He could also see that May wasn't about to confide in him, of all people, exactly where she had been, or who she had really seen this morning.

He grimaced. 'January isn't going to thank you for inviting me to dinner.'

May shrugged. 'If you hadn't noticed, my youngest sister isn't very happy with me at the moment, anyway.' She sighed. 'My consorting with the enemy isn't going to make that any worse than it already is!'

Max winced. 'The enemy? Is that really how you all see me?'

It wasn't a very pleasant feeling, he had to admit. Oh, not all of the deals he had completed on Jude's behalf over the years had been easy, or indeed amicable, but he had never actually seen himself as the enemy before!

It wasn't a feeling he liked.

'Come to dinner, Max,' May dismissed laughingly. 'I'm cooking roast chicken,' she told him enticingly. 'I'm sure a home-cooked meal isn't something you have too often,' she added ruefully.

This woman, Max was slowly realizing, saw altogether too much. God help the man who tried to make *her* his own!

CHAPTER EIGHT

'YOU'VE done what?' January stared at her eldest sister incredulously.

'I said you need to lay four places at the table for dinner because I've invited Max to eat with us this evening,' May repeated calmly as she continued to stir the gravy. 'In fact, he should be here any minute.'

That was what January had thought she'd said! 'Have you gone completely mad, May?' she gasped.

May grimaced. 'Not as far as I'm aware, no. Look,' her sister continued firmly as she could see January was about to disagree with her, 'isn't it better to—to, well, get to know Max a little, let him get to know us in return? It's much harder to walk all over someone if you actually know them personally,' she reasoned impatiently as January continued to look furious.

January gave a disgusted snort. 'Max doesn't seem to be having too much trouble with that so far!'

She really couldn't believe May had invited Max to dinner. Or that Max had accepted the invitation…!

He had to know, couldn't fail to appreciate, that he was as welcome here as a rampaging bull! That he actually proposed to be more destructive than that bull!

As for May…!

'I think you're wrong about that, January,' her sister said consideringly. 'In fact, I sense a distinct wavering in his resolve to get us out of here,' she added happily.

January shook her head. 'Then you can see more than I can! March is going to think you've gone completely off your trolley, too,' she assured her with satisfaction.

Her eldest sister shrugged. 'Let's just wait and see, shall we?' she murmured enigmatically.

'You can, if you like,' January snapped, pointedly laying three places at the table. 'I would rather eat out!'

'January—'

'Whew, what a lousy evening!' March complained as she swept into the kitchen, bringing a blast of cold air and falling snow in with her. 'And talking of lousy evenings—look who I met outside!' She stepped aside to reveal Max standing in the doorway behind her.

January stared at him, still unable to believe May seriously expected her to calmly sit down and eat dinner with him. Or that he should dare to sit down to dinner with them!

Was he so insensitive? Could he not see how unwelcome he was here? Could he not see how much she didn't want him here?

'Shut the door, for goodness' sake,' May advised briskly. 'It looks as if it's getting worse out there,' she added frowningly after glancing out of the kitchen window.

'It is,' March confirmed ruefully. 'I wouldn't send a dog out there again tonight,' she added dryly, raising mocking brows in Max's direction. 'Do you intend staying long, Mr Golding?' she prompted pointedly.

Trust March to get straight to the heart of the matter, January acknowledged admiringly, at the same time shooting May a triumphant look.

'Max is my guest, March,' May reproved softly.

'Really?' March looked impressed.

Impressed wasn't exactly the way January felt about this situation! Although March's comment about the worsening weather pretty well put paid to her own idea of going out for the evening!

'In that case, I had better go up and change before dinner,' March taunted.

'Don't bother on my account.' Max spoke for the first time since his arrival. 'May assured me it would be an informal evening,' he added with a glance down at his own casual trousers and what looked like a blue cashmere sweater beneath his thick outer jacket.

The humour increased in March's hazel grey-green eyes. 'I'm going to dress down, Mr Golding, not up,' she told him laughingly before leaving the room.

'Keep an eye on the gravy for me, will you, January?' May asked distractedly as she followed March up the stairs.

Leaving January completely alone in the kitchen with Max. Great! Just what she had wanted!

'Did May tell you I would be here this evening?' he prompted, his sharp gaze passing briefly over the three places set at the table.

January glared at him. 'We were just—discussing it, when you arrived,' she bit out tautly.

His mouth twisted self-derisively. 'What you really mean is that you were making it clear you aren't exactly thrilled at my coming here,' he accepted mockingly.

'You knew I wouldn't be,' she snapped impatiently, moving to noisily lay the missing fourth place at the table. 'How could you?' She turned to glare at him. 'What do you think you're hoping to achieve? Because May—bless her!—may have been won over by you, for some inexplicable reason, but I can assure you that March and I aren't fooled for a moment!'

He gave an admiring glance upstairs. 'She's something else, isn't she?' he murmured smilingly.

'May or March?' she challenged disgustedly.

'Both of them, actually.' He smiled. 'For different reasons, of course.'

'Oh, of course,' January agreed sarcastically—not having the least idea what he meant! She hardly knew May at the moment, so illogical was her behaviour, although March—thank goodness—was her usual sharp-tongued self.

'I bought a peace-offering.' Max held up the bottle of wine he had been holding the whole time he'd stood beside the closed kitchen door. 'May mentioned we were having chicken, so...' He moved to place the bottle of white wine on the table. 'It's already chilled enough,' he added dryly.

January looked at him frustratedly. 'Why are you here, Max?'

He shrugged. 'May invited me.'

She gave a dazed shake of her head. 'You know, when we were younger, I was always the one who brought home the wounded birds and animals, May was always the one who warned me they wouldn't survive away from their own environment. Their own kind,' she added pointedly.

His gaze was narrowed now, that nerve once again pulsing in his tightly clenched jaw. 'I hope you're not implying that I'm wounded in some way?' he finally bit out harshly.

Her eyes flashed impatiently. 'I was implying that you should stay with your own kind!' Obviously her sarcasm was completely lost on this man! But then, she hadn't had as much practice at it as March had. But that didn't mean she couldn't learn...

Max's brow cleared, his smile rueful now. 'And exactly what is my own kind, January?'

'Predatory!' she answered with satisfaction.

He gave a disarming grin. 'I have a feeling that any man would find himself completely outgunned—as well as outnumbered—by the three Calendar sisters!'

January did her best to maintain her furious expression—and failed miserably as her lips twitched and she began to smile, too. What was it about this man? How could she start off being angry or distant with him—usually angry!—and then end up grinning at him like an idiot? It didn't make any sense!

'January,' he murmured softly, crossing the room to stand in front of her, his hands moving up to gently cradle each side of her face as he looked down at her searchingly. 'I really thought it might have been you who was attacked last night,' he groaned huskily.

Her breath caught in her throat. 'And that would have bothered you?'

A frown darkened his brow. 'Of course it would have bothered me!' he rasped. 'You must have known that…?' He looked down at her frustratedly, fingers lightly caressing her brows.

She gave a shake of her head. 'I'm not sure what I know any more, Max. One minute you're—you're making love to me, and the next—! Well, we both know what happened next,' she remembered hardly, deliberately moving away, his hands falling back to his sides.

Just in time, as it happened, her two sisters coming back into the kitchen at that moment, May's sharp gaze instantly taking in the fact that the two of them stood well apart, the tension between them tangible.

'March was just telling me that there's been another

attack,' May said briskly as she moved to check the food cooking on top of the Aga.

'I meant to tell you earlier,' January groaned. 'But I—it slipped my mind.' She deliberately avoided looking at Max—because they both knew he was the reason she had forgotten to mention this latest attack to her sister.

'I meant to tell you all when I came in,' March muttered self-disgustedly. 'But for some reason it slipped my mind, too.' She gave Max a pointed grimace, having changed into black denims and a bright orange jumper, the latter eye-catching, to say the least.

'There seems to be a lot of it about,' Max murmured appreciatively.

'Yes,' March drawled wryly.

'Tell them the worst part about it, March,' May encouraged impatiently.

'What—? Oh, yes.' March nodded. 'It was Josh,' she announced slightly incredulously.

'What was?' January prompted dazedly, still confused from having Max touch her in that way. Would she ever understand him?

'Josh…?' Max repeated slowly. 'The same Josh who is marrying your cousin—Sara, isn't it?—on Saturday?' He looked accusingly at January, the sharpness of that gaze reminding her that it was the same Josh who had kissed her on Saturday evening!

'That's the one,' March confirmed. 'Although I'm not sure if the wedding will still be going ahead, in the circumstances?' She looked across at May.

'I'll telephone Aunt Lyn in a moment.' May nodded. 'How awful for them all.' She shook her head distractedly.

'Hang on a minute,' January protested, having been

listening to this conversation with increasing incredulity.

She had known Josh most of her life, had, as she'd told Max on Saturday, been at school with him, and while there was no doubting Josh could be a little boisterous at times, liked to have fun, he also didn't have a vicious bone in his body.

'They have to have the wrong man.' She shook her head dismissively. 'Josh isn't capable of attacking anyone, let alone seven women.'

'Oh, no, you misunderstood me,' March apologized with a grimace. 'Josh was the one who was attacked,' she explained disgustedly. 'Beaten up pretty badly, from what I gather.'

What the hell—?

Now Max was as confused as January looked. Although, he had to admit, a few seconds ago he had been angry with her at her defence of the other man…!

'But he's a man!' January burst out incredulously.

As well she might. As far as Max had been able to gather—although, having been out of the country for several months, he was obviously a latecomer to these random attacks—all the other victims had been women.

'Are they sure it was the Night Striker?' He frowned his own puzzlement.

'Positive,' March confirmed, seeming to have forgotten her antagonism towards him—for the moment. 'Same M.O., or whatever they call it.' She grimaced.

'Modus operandi,' Max murmured frowningly. 'Latin,' he explained as he glanced up to find all three sisters looking at him.

March nodded, her gaze mocking. 'Being a lawyer, you would know that.'

His mouth twisted. 'I wouldn't be a very good one if I didn't.'

'And we're all sure that you're very good,' March taunted.

'Thank you,' he accepted dryly, easily guessing it wasn't meant as a compliment; March was more sharp-tongued than he was himself. 'I accept that the method may be the same,' he acknowledged slowly. 'But the fact that the victim was a man this time makes it totally different.'

In fact, it didn't make much sense to him. Okay, so the last six victims, all women, had been badly beaten rather than raped, but that still didn't explain why it had been a man who was attacked this time… The good-natured Josh, of all people. No wonder the police were being a little cagey about the information they gave out!

'Sara must be so upset,' January said worriedly.

As Max might have known she would; of the three sisters, January was definitely the most empathetic.

'If none of you mind waiting for dinner, I'll telephone Aunt Lyn now and see how Josh is. And Sara, of course,' May murmured distractedly before leaving the room.

'And I'll open the wine,' Max suggested briskly, seeing that a certain amount of shock was starting to set in with all the sisters now; hearing of the attacks the last six months couldn't have been very pleasant, having it arrive on their own doorstep, so to speak, must be even more shocking. 'Could you get me a corkscrew, January?' he said briskly as neither sister moved.

'Oh. Of course.' She moved frowningly to one of

the drawers, taking out the corkscrew to hand it to him distractedly.

'And some glasses, March?' he prompted lightly as he deftly removed the cork.

March blinked, her smile derisive as she seemed to guess what he was doing. 'Certainly, sir,' she drawled, reaching up to take four wineglasses from one of the cabinets.

'Thank you,' Max accepted dryly, starting to pour the wine.

'You're welcome,' March derided. 'Mmm,' she murmured appreciatively after her first sip of the wine. 'Just what we need to cheer us all up.'

'Maybe I should have brought two bottles,' Max teased.

'Maybe you should.' March nodded, grey-green eyes dancing with humour.

'January?' Max prompted as she made no effort to pick up one of the glasses.

In fact, she seemed totally distracted, he acknowledged with a searching frown, her face unnaturally pale, her eyes so deep a grey they looked almost black.

It was awful that their cousin's future husband had been the Night Striker's latest victim, but unless Max was mistaken, January seemed more stunned by it than her sisters…?

'I still can't believe it.' She shook her head before picking up her glass of wine and taking a sip.

For all the notice she took of its delicate taste and fragrance he might as well have brought a bottle of cheap plonk!

'There must have been some sort of mistake,' January said. 'I can't believe anyone could have deliberately set out to hurt Josh. He's just so nice, so unassuming; as far as I'm aware, he doesn't have an enemy in the world—' She broke off, a stricken look on her face now as she slowly turned to look at Max.

It was a look Max didn't like one little bit!

Surely January couldn't think—didn't believe—

'January?' he prompted harshly.

'Yes?' She swallowed hard, looking more bewildered than ever now.

'March, would you leave us for a few minutes?' Max requested, his gaze still fixed icily on January.

'January?' March prompted softly.

'I—yes. Fine.' January nodded dazedly, her gaze studiously avoiding Max's now.

'In that case, I think I'll go and see how May is getting on,' March drawled before leaving.

Max moved to stand in front of January, his hand under her chin as he tilted her face up to his, forcing her to look at him. And he didn't like what he saw in her eyes!

'You don't seriously think *I* had anything to do with this attack on Josh?' he rasped disbelievingly.

Because he could clearly see that the possibility had definitely crossed her mind—if only briefly!

Although it was starting to fade now, that bewilderment fading from her eyes, too. To be replaced by self-derision. 'No, of course I don't.' She gave a firm shake of her head. 'Of course not,' she added more strongly.

His hands moved to her shoulders as he shook her slightly. 'I bought the man a drink, for goodness' sake,' he ground out. 'He bought me one, too!' He tightened his hands painfully on her shoulders, furious that the thought could have crossed her mind, even for a minute.

But he knew that it had, no matter what January might claim to the contrary.

And could he really blame her? He had been blowing hot and cold with her from the moment they'd met, his actions appearing completely illogical. One evening he had been prepared to knock Josh to the ground for daring to kiss January, and the next evening, following his discovery of exactly who she was, of how dangerous she was to his own personal equilibrium, he had mocked her for responding to him. Not exactly consistent, was he?

Nevertheless, he found her suspicion of him, even for that brief moment, very unsettling… And hurtful…?

January was smiling now, albeit ruefully. 'No doubt that alone was enough to make the two of you bosom buddies!'

His mouth tightened. 'Not necessarily,' he allowed, realizing how ridiculous his claim must have sounded; the fact that the two had bought each other a drink did not change the fact that seconds earlier Max had been about to hit the other man! His hands dropped away from her shoulders as he stepped back. 'No matter what you may think to the contrary, I am not a violent man. Perhaps I had better leave—'

'Please don't leave on my account,' January cut in awkwardly. 'I—I'm sorry.' She pushed the darkness of her hair back from her face. 'I'm just a little—upset.' She grimaced.

He could see that, and he was sorry for it. But, at the moment, he had to admit to being just a little upset himself! With himself, mainly, for having behaved in such a way as to have given January even the briefest of doubts where he was concerned.

He shook his head. 'I still think it might be better if I left—'

'Who's leaving?' March prompted lightly as she came back into the room.

'I am,' Max told her forcefully. 'I believe I've already outstayed my welcome!' he added hardly.

March grimaced as she gave a shake of her head. 'That may or may not be the case, but I somehow don't think you'll be leaving us just yet,' she informed him ruefully. 'I just listened to the news on television; the snowstorm has turned into a blizzard,' she explained at his questioning look. 'They are advising all drivers in the area to stay at home, if at all possible.'

Home.

It was a long time since he had had one of those. If, indeed, he ever really had. But the Calendar farm was certainly far from being that to him!

'I'm afraid March is right, Max,' May assured him as she came back into the room. 'I asked Aunt Lyn if it was possible for us to visit Josh later this evening. She assured me that it was, but that there had been a warning given out for people not to travel. March turned on the news and—I'm afraid you won't be going anywhere tonight, Max,' she informed him lightly.

His narrowed gaze moved questioningly to January—just in time for him to see the look of dismay on her face she wasn't quick enough to hide!

CHAPTER NINE

'THIS is really very good of you.'

January turned to look at Max as he stood in the doorway watching her make up the bed he was to sleep in.

And it wasn't very good of her at all. She knew it wasn't. And so did he.

She still couldn't believe those brief feelings of suspicion she had had about him earlier. Worse, couldn't believe she had let Max see those suspicions.

Of course he wasn't responsible for the attack on Josh. Yes, Max had been angry at the younger man on Saturday when Josh had dared to kiss her, had looked more than capable of hitting Josh when he'd pulled him away from January. But on Sunday evening, the very next day, Max had made it more than plain that she would never be more than a brief flirtation to him. Rather nullifying any feelings of violence he might have previously felt towards Josh!

She drew in a deep breath before straightening, facing Max across the width of her father's bedroom. 'I really do apologise for—well, for any thoughts I may have had earlier—'

'That I'm the person who attacked Josh?' Max finished scathingly as he strolled further into the room. 'If it makes you feel any better, January, I'm sure the police will have been informed about my—little disagreement, with Josh on Saturday evening, and will be following it up accordingly. They will no doubt be questioning me about the incident,' he explained dryly as she looked puzzled.

January could feel her cheeks paling. She hadn't thought of that.

How awful.

But no more awful, surely, than those brief suspicions she had had concerning Max?

'Was this your father's bedroom?'

She turned back to Max, to see him looking interestedly around the room, her father's brush and comb set still on the dressing table, along with several paperback books, a photograph of the three sisters taking pride of place beside the clock on the bedside cabinet.

Max reached out to pick up the photograph, studying it for several long moments, before putting it carefully back in place. 'Cute,' he murmured.

January turned away. She had been feeling awkward with him all evening. As the four of them had eaten dinner together. As they'd turned the television on later that evening to listen to the weather forecast and heard that the blizzard had now spread over most of the country. The warning had been repeated about not travelling unless it was absolutely necessary, accompanied by several scenes where people hadn't heeded that warning, showing dozens of vehicles that had had to be abandoned.

The least she could do, January had decided, was to offer to make up Max's bed for the night.

'I hope you don't mind?' She indicated the bedroom. 'The only other bed we have available is in the small bedsit we had converted over the garage—and that hasn't been used since the summer.' She grimaced.

Max looked at her with narrowed eyes. 'That would

be the accommodation used by the help you had staying last summer?'

January gave him a sharp look. How did he—? Of course, she and May had discussed that in front of him earlier today. Although she sensed more than casual interest in Max's remark…?

'Yes,' she confirmed slowly, watching him warily now.

His mouth twisted ruefully. 'I wouldn't have thought you would particularly care whether or not I froze to death over there.'

Of course she cared. Too much, as it happened.

She shrugged. 'That may be a little difficult to explain to anyone who comes looking for you,' she returned tartly.

He grimaced. 'That's always supposing that someone did.'

January gave a humourless smile. 'I'm sure Jude Marshall would wonder what had happened to his lawyer!'

Max had once again picked up the photograph of the three sisters, glancing across at her. 'He just might at that,' he conceded dryly. 'You were very young when this photograph was taken.' He frowned down at the image.

'About two and a half.' January nodded, strolling over to look down at the photograph. 'March was three and a half, May a little over four.'

'Three peas in a pod,' Max drawled, referring to what January had said was her father's description of them. 'There seems to be someone standing behind you,' he continued frowningly. 'There, you see.' He pointed to the hand resting on May's left shoulder and another on March's right, January sandwiched between her two sisters. 'Your father?' he prompted interestedly.

She shook her head. 'My father took the photograph.'

Max looked even more puzzled. 'Then who—?'

'My mother,' she told him abruptly, taking the photograph out of his hand and returning it to its original place on the bedside cabinet.

Max looked at her frowningly. 'Your mother? But—'

'Can I get you anything else before I go to bed myself?' January cut in briskly. 'A cup of coffee? Something else to eat?'

'No, thanks,' he answered slowly, once again looking at the photograph of the three sisters. 'Isn't that a little strange?' he murmured softly. 'Why would your mother have been cut from the photograph? Surely it must have been one of the last pictures your father had of the four of you together?'

'Probably, yes,' January confirmed sharply, not welcoming his questions.

Because she had asked her father the same question once. His answer that the photograph wouldn't fit into the frame if it wasn't cut down had seemed very strange, even to an eight-year-old. But the look on her father's face, almost of bewilderment, had been enough for her never to ask about her mother again.

Max was looking at her searchingly now, his brow clearing as he answered her previous question, 'I really don't need anything else, thanks,' he repeated lightly. 'And don't worry, January,' he added dryly. 'I promise I'll be out of your way as soon as the weather breaks.'

'That's good,' she answered distractedly, her expression instantly becoming stricken as she realized exactly what she had said. 'What I meant—'

'I know what you meant, January.' Max laughed softly, moving to stand in front of her, blue eyes gleaming with laughter. 'You meant exactly what you said!' He shook his head. 'And I can't say I exactly blame you,' he added ruefully. 'If I were in your shoes I would feel exactly the same way!'

This wasn't helping January in her efforts to dislike him! Neither was his close proximity!

But maybe May had been right after all; maybe getting to know them all personally—some more than others, January acknowledged with an inner wince!—was making this as difficult for Max as it was for them? She certainly hoped so!

'I'll see you in the morning,' she told him distantly as she moved away determinedly.

'Aren't you going to tuck me in and give me a goodnight kiss?' Max prompted huskily.

'No,' she drawled, turning back to look at him, dark brows raised derisively. 'I'm not going to offer to read you a bedtime story, either!'

'Pity,' he teased, sitting down on the side of the double bed. 'I would like to come with you tomorrow, by the way,' he added seriously.

'Come with me where?' January was having a little trouble keeping up with the jumps in the conversation.

'To see Josh, of course,' he dismissed. 'You will be going in to see him tomorrow, won't you?'

'If the weather breaks,' she confirmed slowly. 'Max, are you sure it's a good idea for you—? What are you doing?' she gasped as he crossed the room in two strides, his fingers biting into her shoulders as he held her in front of him.

'January, I will tell you once more—and once more only!' he warned harshly, shaking her slightly, his eyes glittering darkly. 'I did not—I repeat, not!—have anything to do with the attack on Josh.'

'I don't— Max, you're hurting me!' she gasped at the pressure of his fingers against her shoulders.

He scowled darkly. 'At this moment I would like to very thoroughly beat you,' he told her gratingly. 'But as I've already assured you I am not a violent man—!' His mouth came down fiercely on hers.

His kiss was full of the anger he refused to express in any other way, and January met that anger with the tenderness she longed to give him but daredn't show him in any other way…

It was that tenderness that finally won through, Max groaning low in his throat, his hands cradling each side of her face as he now sipped from the softness of her lips.

Finally he raised his head, his forehead damp against hers as he looked down at her. 'You are the most extraordinary woman I have ever met,' he murmured dazedly.

January moistened her lips before answering, 'I am?'

'Hmm.' He nodded, grimacing slightly, obviously not at all happy with the fact. 'One moment you're thinking I'm some sort of crazed attacker, and the next you're kissing me—'

'Max, you didn't let me finish what I was going to say earlier,' she said huskily, one hand reaching up to briefly touch the hardness of his suddenly clenched jaw. 'I was merely going to ask whether, in the circumstances of your connection to the Marshall Corporation, it was wise for you to come with me to visit Josh. Whether you should become any more involved with my family,' she explained softly as he still frowned.

'I think your warning is probably a little late,' he acknowledged self-derisively. 'And I have every intention of going to see Josh. Maybe he got a look at the person who attacked him. Maybe—'

'Max, I'm sure the police are perfectly capable of dealing with that,' January cut in pointedly. 'After all, you're a lawyer, not a policeman,' she reasoned lightly.

He shook his head. 'There's something wrong with this attack on Josh. Something other than the fact that it was a man this time rather than a woman,' he added wryly at January's knowing look.

'Max—' She broke off as a knock sounded on the bedroom door.

Obviously one of her sisters. Probably wondering why it was taking her so long to make up the bed!

She gave Max a rueful grimace as she moved out of his arms. 'Come in,' she invited dryly, giving her eldest sister a knowing look as she opened the door. 'I was just making sure Max has everything he needs for the night,' she told May teasingly.

May's green gaze flickered reprovingly over Max before moving back to January. 'And does he?'

'As much as an unexpected guest can expect.' Max was the one to answer derisively.

May returned his gaze unblinkingly. 'If you want them, you will find some laundered pyjamas in the top drawer of the dresser.'

'I always sleep in the nude, but thanks anyway,' Max returned tauntingly.

May gave a tight smile. 'You might find the farmhouse a little cooler than you're used to.'

'Not so far,' he came back, dark brows raised challengingly.

'May, I think we'll leave Max to get settled for the night,' January cut in determinedly, having decided this verbal battle of wills had gone on long enough.

'We're usually all up by about six o'clock,' May told Max pointedly.

He nodded, blue eyes dancing with merriment. 'A cup of tea in bed about then will be very welcome!'

May gave a snort of dismissal. 'Guest or not, if we don't have that luxury, then neither do you!'

He shrugged. 'I would be quite happy to bring you all a cup of tea in bed.'

May's gaze narrowed. 'I'll just bet you would—'

'He's winding you up, May,' January cut in once again, shaking her head reprovingly at Max even as she chuckled softly. 'But if you should get the urge to make an early cup of tea, Max, we all take ours without sugar!' she added even as she pushed her sister towards the door. 'You were the one who invited him here in the first place,' she reminded May lightly once they were outside the bedroom, the door safely closed behind them.

'I may have done,' May snapped. 'But I told you why that was. I certainly didn't think he had the nerve to try to seduce my little sister right under my nose!' she added indignantly.

'Your little sister is twenty-five years old,' January reminded her dryly. 'And I'm more than capable of taking care of myself.'

May shook her head. 'Not where Max Golding is concerned, I've just realized,' she said slowly. 'January, are you serious—?'

'Could we leave this for tonight, May?' she cut in

firmly, her earlier humour having completely disappeared. 'I'm really not in the mood to discuss Max any more tonight,' she added heavily.

May looked at her searchingly for several long minutes, before slowly nodding her head. 'Okay,' she agreed huskily. 'But just—never mind.' She shook her head, smiling. 'Everything will look different in the morning,' she added brightly.

January was glad her sister had said different, and not better. Because somehow January doubted it would be that. In the morning she would still be in love with Max. And that couldn't be good. For any of them.

Considering he had doubted that he would sleep at all, with January so close and yet so unattainable, Max found he had slept for almost eight hours, a glance at his wrist-watch telling him it was almost seven o'clock.

Way past time for taking January—or anyone else!—a cup of tea in bed!

He smiled as he imagined May's indignation if he had arrived in the sisters' bedrooms with the suggested morning tea. Whatever had prompted the eldest Calendar sister to invite him to dinner last night, May had definitely changed her mind about the wisdom of that invitation by the time she'd come looking for January in this bedroom later in the evening.

Wisely so, Max acknowledged with a self-derisive grimace.

No matter what he did, how hard he tried to keep a distance between himself and January, to concentrate on the business side of their relationship rather than the personal, he invariably ended up kissing her instead!

Maybe—

He heard a door slam downstairs, followed by muffled noises outside, evidence that the sisters were indeed up and about. And May, at least, was no doubt frowning disapprovingly about his own tardiness in getting up!

She was also right about the coldness of the farmhouse, he discovered a few minutes later as he hurriedly dressed before going to the bathroom across the hall, the tiles in there ultra cold on his sock-covered feet.

And the most he had to compare this cold discomfort with was the times he went skiing, when he spent his evenings and nights in a wonderfully warm ski lodge, his days wrapped up warmly as he skied the slopes. Hardly any comparison at all!

You're getting soft, Golding, he told himself disgustedly, at the same time acknowledging that he was ill-equipped to survive in conditions like these. Which also made him wonder why on earth the Calendar sisters would want to…!

Only May and March were in evidence when he entered the kitchen a few minutes later, this room much warmer than the rest of the house, Max realized thankfully.

'Coffee?' March offered abruptly as she held up the steaming pot invitingly.

'Thanks.' He nodded distractedly, aware of May's brooding silence as she sat at the kitchen table drinking her own warm brew, studiously ignoring him, it seemed.

'Help yourself to milk and sugar,' March told him dismissively as she placed a mug of coffee on the table for him. 'In case you're wondering, January is over in the shed dealing with early milking,' she added dryly.

Was he really that obvious? Max wondered with a

scowl. Probably, he conceded heavily. To January's sisters, at least…

'Now that we've cleared the drifts away from the doors and a path over to the shed,' May put in pointedly.

While he lingered in his bed trying to build up the courage to get out of the warmth of the bedclothes into the cold of the room, May implied, but didn't actually say.

'Is there anything I can do to help?' he offered—and as quickly realized how ridiculous he sounded; what on earth did he know about any of the workings of a farm?

March obviously found the offer just as ridiculous, giving a wry smile. 'Stay out of everyone's way?' she suggested scathingly.

Feeling inadequate did not sit easily on Max's shoulders; having it pointed out to him by the more outspoken of the Calendar sisters only made it worse!

He stood up noisily. 'I think I'll just go over anyway and see if there's anything I can do for January.'

May sat back, looking at him derisively. 'I think you've already done enough for her, don't you?' she murmured enigmatically.

Max's gaze narrowed on her speculatively as he pulled on his heavy jacket. Obviously whatever headway he had made with May yesterday had been completely voided by having January linger in the bedroom with him last night, May definitely back to her old protective self.

Family disapproval was also something Max had never encountered before—mainly because he had never so much as suggested meeting any of the family of the women he had been involved with over the years!

God, he really had to get out of here. And not just the farmhouse, either!

Which may prove a little difficult, he discovered on opening the door; May really hadn't been joking about the snowdrifts! They were as high as four feet along the side of the shed and the hedgerow of the track up here to the house.

'Our uncle—Sara's father—is going to come up from the road and clear it later this morning,' March assured him with a mocking grin—obviously having enjoyed the look of dismay on his face for several minutes first.

Max didn't even bother to reply as he closed the door behind him, pausing in the porch to pull on his walking boots before staggering across to the cow shed. And it really was staggering, the ground extremely slippery underfoot. But at least the snow seemed to have stopped falling.

Quite what he had expected once inside the shed, he really had no idea. But it certainly wasn't to hear the sounds of the electric milking machines—or to see January as he had never seen her before!

Faded denims were tucked into knee-high wellington boots, a coat that looked several sizes too big for her reaching warmly down to her knees, a scarf muffled up about her face, her ebony hair all but hidden beneath a multicoloured woolen hat.

Grey eyes—the only part of her face visible!—were full of laughter as she looked up and saw his astounded expression.

She pulled the scarf down from over her mouth,

grinning ruefully. 'See what I mean about the impracticality of love at first sight!' she derided.

Max recovered quickly, the beautiful grey eyes the same, as was her smile. 'This certainly beats the toothpaste tube and the bare feet,' he acknowledged dryly, moving further into the shed.

It was warmer in here than outside, probably because of the heat given off by the animals themselves. Although there were other disadvantages, the animals giving off a smell that was overwhelming.

He grimaced. 'May still seems a little—annoyed with me, this morning.'

'With you, too?' January shrugged. 'She'll get over it.'

Max was still curious as to where the elder Calendar sister had been when she'd claimed she was going to the dentist. But as neither of her sisters seemed to have the least suspicion, and May herself was completely unforthcoming, he didn't think he stood much chance of finding out.

'I'll be finished in here soon, if you would like to go back to the house,' January offered. 'Unless, of course, it really is a little too frosty over there?' She quirked dark brows teasingly.

'I'm sure I can cope,' Max drawled. 'But I'll wait for you, anyway.'

In actual fact, he quite enjoyed watching January's dexterous movements as she finished milking the first set of cows before moving on to the next.

He also couldn't help smiling as he imagined the faces of the guests staying at the hotel if they could see the glamorous singer from the piano-bar now. January's gorgeous figure was completely hidden in the bulky clothing she wore, and, as far as he could tell, she didn't have on even a dusting of make-up, not even a lip gloss.

And yet she was still beautiful to him, he realized somewhat dazedly. What was happening to him?

It certainly wasn't the right time for his mobile telephone to start ringing. Mainly because he could too easily guess who the caller was going to be!

Despite the time difference between here and America, Max knew from experience that Jude was a man who needed very little sleep—and who didn't appreciate that others might not be quite so fortunate!

'Shouldn't you get that?' January prompted curiously as he made no effort to take the intrusive telephone from his pocket.

He shrugged. 'If it's important, I'm sure they will call back.'

But as the telephone kept ringing Max was more convinced than ever that the caller had to be Jude; the other man really didn't take no for an answer! Besides, when hadn't Max been available to take Jude's calls?

He looked about his surroundings self-derisively. When standing in the middle of a cow shed, with the woman who was slowly driving him insane, that was when!

CHAPTER TEN

JANUARY gave an inner sigh of relief as Max's attention was distracted when he finally decided to answer the call. Despite her earlier self-derision, it had been very unnerving having him standing there watching her as she worked.

For one thing, for all this was her usual garb when she was working on the farm, she looked so unglamorous. For another, she was still so aware of the fact that she couldn't be alone with this man for longer than two minutes without ending up in his arms!

Not that she thought there was much chance of that happening at the moment—Max would need to be blind as well as besotted to find her attractive the way she looked right now. And January knew he was neither of those things…

'Don't you ever sleep, Jude?' she heard him snap into the mobile telephone.

Jude…? Jude Marshall?

'Jude, I believe we had this same conversation yesterday,' he bit out irritably.

About the three of them, no doubt, January acknowledged resentfully, unashamedly listening to Max's side of the conversation now even while she gave every appearance of continuing with the milking.

'They simply do not want to sell, Jude,' Max rasped. 'That is, of course, your prerogative,' he continued coldly. 'No. No, I don't. I—' He broke off as one of the cows gave an extremely loud moo in the background. 'What was that?' he obviously repeated the question that had been put to him, giving January a brief grimace before replying. 'I have the television on, Jude,' he invented. 'The news. Look, Jude, I'm sure you didn't telephone me at this ridiculous hour, wasting your time and money, to talk about what I may or may not be watching on television! But for your information, we've had snowstorms here—Yes, snowstorms! I am freezing cold, and not a little fed up with this whole situation—' He listened for a few seconds. 'So fire me!' he snapped before abruptly ending the call.

January stared at him. Had he really just told the owner of the Marshall Corporation, his friend as well as employer, what he could do with his job? And if so, why had he…?

'Don't look so worried,' Max drawled as he looked up and saw January's stunned expression. 'Jude won't fire me,' he sighed. 'We go too far back for him to ever do that.'

So that challenge had just been bravado on his part? January could hardly contain her disappointment. For a moment there she had really thought—

The mobile telephone began to ring a second time. Obviously Jude Marshall wasn't a man used to taking no for an answer.

Well—obviously, January instantly chided herself, otherwise Max wouldn't be here in the first place. Something she would do well to keep remembering; Max was only here to try and persuade her and her sisters into selling their home.

If only she didn't love him so much!

'January?'

She lowered long lashes over her eyes, determined

that Max wouldn't see her tears. Let him play his stupid power games with Jude Marshall—and leave her alone.

'Shouldn't you answer that?' she said huskily as he came to stand in front of her, the ringing mobile telephone still in his hand.

'I can talk to Jude any time,' Max rasped, the ringing ceasing abruptly as he switched it off. 'January—'

'I'm really very busy, Max.' She moved purposefully away from him as he would have reached out and taken her in his arms—so much for thinking she looked undesirable! 'And you're cold,' she reminded him determinedly. 'My uncle should have cleared the track shortly, so you'll be able to drive back to the hotel,' she added dismissively, her chin rising challengingly. 'Maybe even book yourself a flight back to America, away from this cold weather,' she added scathingly.

A nerve pulsed in his tightly clenched jaw. 'Is that what you want?' he muttered grimly.

'Of course,' she assured him brightly. 'We all just want to get on with our lives. Don't you?' she derided.

His eyes glittered. 'My life isn't in America!' he snapped.

'Well, wherever it is, then,' January shrugged, wishing he would just go—before those threatening tears began to fall.

She simply couldn't bear the thought of Max going completely out of her life, of never seeing him again.

Max stared at her for several long minutes, his expression grim. 'Okay,' he finally muttered forcefully. 'I'll go back to the farmhouse and wait for your uncle. But I'm still coming with you later to see Josh,' he warned hardly.

January gave a weary shrug. 'I doubt I could stop you even if I wanted to.'

His gaze narrowed. 'And do you want to?'

'Max,' she began impatiently, 'as far as you're concerned, what I do or don't want doesn't seem to be particularly important,' she snapped. 'Now, if you wouldn't mind; I'm busy,' she added rudely before turning away, hearing the slam of the shed door seconds later.

Her shoulders slumped wearily after his departure, the tears falling hot on her cheeks. Well, she hadn't ended up in his arms being kissed this time, had she? No, this time she had told him she just wanted him to leave, not just the farm, but the country!

And, with him as Jude Marshall's representative, she most certainly did want that. But as the man she had fallen in love with—!

She had thought herself in love with Ben last year, had been so hurt when she'd found out that the real motive behind his interest in her, with her father now dead, was with an eye to the farm. Not for the redevelopment Jude Marshall had in mind—just as owner by marriage to one of the sisters. That was probably what had hurt January the most when she'd finally got the full story from him: the fact that he had tried it on with her two sisters, and been kindly but firmly rejected, before turning his attention to the youngest sister. And like an idiot she had fallen for it!

Just as she had fallen for Max, she reminded herself derisively.

Yes, and even knowing the full circumstances of his presence here, she still loved Max. He would just never know that she did.

Perhaps, after all, the sooner Max left the area, the better it would be. For everyone. But certainly for January.

Which was the main reason she was so cool towards him that evening when the two of them finally managed to visit Josh.

Not that it was easy to get in to see her cousin-in-law-to-be, a certain amount of police security around him still, but luckily her Aunt Lyn had already left word to expect at least one of the sisters in this evening.

In fact, January was glad in the end that she had Max with her, so shocked was she at Josh's changed appearance. Someone had really beaten him badly, a large discoloured gash on his left temple that had obviously needed several stitches, a huge bruise on his jaw, one of his arms in a sling.

'Hi,' he greeted brightly enough. 'You just missed seeing Sara; I finally managed to persuade her that I wasn't going to die if she went home for a bath and change of clothes,' he explained ruefully. 'Hello again.' He gave Max a smile, although it obviously caused him pain.

January bent to give Josh a kiss on the side of his face that didn't look bruised, more shaken than she cared to admit—that someone had deliberately inflicted these wounds. Fights and scenes of violence were so often depicted on television nowadays that it was easy to become hardened to them, but to actually see Josh in this terrible state because someone had deliberately attacked him…!

'Whoever did this ought to be—'

'Don't worry, January, Sara has already said it all,' Josh assured her with a grimace. 'And to think I never knew she had such a violent streak in her until yesterday!' he added affectionately.

'Whereas I already know what January is capable of,' Max put in dryly.

January gave him a sharp look, the colour entering her cheeks as she remembered the visit she had paid him at the hotel on Sunday evening, when she had quite obviously wanted to hit him for what she considered to be his duplicity.

'And they call them the gentler sex!' Josh joined in teasingly. 'Give me a man to fight any day! Although there wasn't too much chance of that on Monday night,' he sobered frowningly. 'The bast— He hit me on the head with something—' he held a hand up to the bruised gash on his temple '—before kicking hell out of me while I was on the ground!'

'Obviously no one told him about the Queensbury Rules,' Max rasped.

Josh gave the other man a grateful smile for his attempt at humour. 'I wouldn't say it was part of his vocabulary, no.'

January sat down abruptly in the chair next to the bed, still shocked that someone could have hurt Josh deliberately.

A group of them had always gone around together at school, January and her cousin Sara, along with several other girls of the same age, Josh and a group of his friends usually around somewhere, too. That something like this should have happened to one of them...!

It was testament to how shocked January was that she did not demur as Max sat down in the chair next to her and took her hand into his own, his fingers tightening reassuringly against hers. In actual fact, at that particular moment other human contact was very welcome.

'Fortunately, Sara has decided that she doesn't mind

me looking like this in the wedding photographs, so the wedding is still on for Saturday,' Josh said lightly. 'They're letting me out of here tomorrow,' he added with satisfaction.

'Any leads as to who did this to you?' Max prompted grimly.

'Not a one,' Josh answered disappointedly. 'The man was wearing a baclava or something, so I couldn't see his face. The only thing I could tell the police that was of any help was that I thought I recognized his voice.'

January's eyes widened incredulously. Josh actually *knew* the man who had done this to him?

'Did it sound anything like mine?' Max suggested dryly.

Josh looked puzzled by the question. 'What?'

'Never mind,' Max dismissed scathingly.

While at the same time not even glancing at January! Leaving her in no doubt that, despite her apology, Max really hadn't forgiven her for even having had that particular thought. But could she blame him…?

'I have no idea where I know it from,' Josh continued frustratedly. 'I've tried and tried to place it, but it just escapes me. I just know that I had heard it before. Somewhere.' He shook his head disgustedly at his own inability to remember.

'It's time for Mr Williams' rest now, I'm afraid,' a nurse looked briefly into the room to inform them.

Josh grimaced. 'I've done nothing but rest since they brought me in here. I shall be glad to get home tomorrow.'

'And I'm sure Sara will be pleased to have you there.' January bent forward to give him another kiss on the cheek before standing up, Max, to her surprise, retaining that hold on her hand as he too stood up to leave.

'Take care,' he told Josh as the two men shook hands.

'See you both on Saturday,' Josh called after them as they left. 'At the wedding.'

Josh was obviously expecting Max to accompany her. But after seeing the two of them here together today, holding hands no less, was that so surprising…?

'Don't look so worried, January,' Max taunted as he saw her frowning expression. 'I'm sure that Josh won't notice my absence amongst all the other wedding guests.'

Damn it, did she have to make it so obvious that she didn't want him there? As if he were some sort of ogre, for goodness' sake. But, then, perhaps to January he was…?

'I'm making it a new rule,' he continued hardly at her silence, 'never to go anywhere I'm not welcome!'

Which just about ruled out the whole of this part of the *country*, if the Calendar sisters had anything to say about it!

'Max—'

'Don't say anything, January,' he snapped as they got outside the hospital. 'I've really had more than enough for one day! I'll see you around,' he added dismissively.

She frowned her confusion. 'Don't you want me to give you a lift back to the hotel?'

To be honest, he had completely forgotten that January had picked him up from there earlier. But it didn't change the fact that he would rather be alone.

'I'll walk,' he assured her abruptly, turning up the

collar on his heavy jacket in an attempt to ward off the chilling wind.

'But—'

'Just leave it, January,' he rasped, blue eyes glittering warningly.

The fact that she flinched at the harshness of his tone, those incredible grey eyes filling up with tears, was almost his undoing. But, at the same time, he was aware that until he knew exactly what he was going to do next, it was better if he just stayed away from January. He couldn't think straight around her anyway!

'Josh is going to be okay, you know,' he told January huskily. 'A bit battered about the edges,' he acknowledged ruefully. 'But he's young, he'll make a full recovery.'

'Physically, yes.' She nodded slowly. 'But—'

'In other ways, too,' Max cut in firmly. 'I'm sure your cousin Sara is going to make sure of that!'

January smiled for what seemed like the first time today. Much to Max's relief. He didn't like the fact that this had made her so unhappy. In fact, he didn't like anything that made January unhappy…

'I have to go,' he repeated harshly. 'Drive back carefully, won't you?' he couldn't resist adding. The roads had been cleared once they'd got down from the farm, but with evening setting in driving was once again hazardous. And he was still recovering from the shock of the last time January ended up in a ditch!

'Of course,' she acknowledged distantly. 'Take care,' she added abruptly before turning sharply away and walking over to where she had parked her sister's car.

Max stood and watched her leave, aware that this might be the last time he saw her. He had some thinking to do, and the outcome of those thoughts might just mean she would get her wish and he would return to America.

She raised a hand in parting as she drove out of the car park, still pale from her shock at Josh's appearance, but also incredibly beautiful.

Max stood on the pavement until the car had completely disappeared from view, reluctant to give up what might be his last view of her.

He had meant it earlier when he'd assured January that Jude would never fire him, but, in view of his personal difficulty over execution of this latest business venture of Jude's, he did wonder if he ought to resign. To do what, he had no idea, but one thing he knew for certain: he was no longer one-hundred-per-cent committed to the Marshall Corporation.

After the years he had spent with the company as the main focus of his life, coming to terms with that was hard to do!

And he needed time, time on his own, to decide exactly what he was going to do next.

Although maybe walking back to the hotel hadn't been such a good idea, he decided ruefully, after trudging through the snow and ice for half an hour in order to get there and needing to lie in a hot bath for an hour or so in order to thaw out.

The telephone rang in his suite as he lay in the bath, but, guessing it was Jude once again, he chose to ignore it. The walk earlier hadn't done anything to help him with the confused thoughts that were tumbling around inside his head!

'Don't you ever go home?' He smiled at John as he walked into the bar a couple of hours later, having decided that a drink was what he needed to thaw him inside as well as out.

The barman grinned. 'I thought this was home!'

Max laughed softly as he ordered his drink. At least John always gave him a warm welcome—which was more than could be said for anyone else in the area!

Although, on reflection, it was pretty sad that the only person here to show him a friendly face was the hotel barman!

John placed the requested glass of whisky in front of him. 'I'm surprised you're still here?'

Max shrugged. 'My business is taking a little longer than I anticipated,' he understated.

He had still come to no real decision about his own future plans, having left his mobile switched off so that Jude couldn't reach him, knowing he needed to think this through without any outside interference.

John grimaced. 'This snow can't be helping. I—uh-oh,' he murmured ruefully. 'Here comes Meridew on the prowl again,' he explained softly as Max looked up at him questioningly. 'I obviously haven't been in the last couple of evenings, but apparently he's been wandering around all week like a bear with a sore head!'

John moved to begin dusting down the shelves behind him, obviously intent on looking busy while the manager of the hotel was 'prowling' around.

'Mr Golding! I trust you are still enjoying your stay with us?'

Max turned to look at Peter Meridew, his gaze narrowing as he saw the other man's bandaged right hand. 'Of course,' he assured the other man smoothly. 'Been in the wars?' He indicated the bandaged hand.

The other man's face became flushed. 'Just a sprain,'

he dismissed abruptly. 'Well, if there's nothing I can do for you…' He turned to leave.

'I didn't say that,' Max called after him softly, a terrible suspicion starting to form in his mind.

Josh had said earlier that he recognized the voice of his attacker, from somewhere, and hadn't Peter Meridew had cause to have words with Josh and his friends for their rowdiness on Saturday evening, plus there was the fact that the manager seemed to be around a lot whenever January was singing in the bar…? Add that to Peter Meridew's bandaged hand, and what had you got—?

Circumstantial evidence was what you had, Max, old lad!

And as a lawyer he ought to know better.

'Yes?' the manager prompted brightly.

Yes—what? He had called out to the other man instinctively, and now he didn't know what to say to him.

'Er— I'm probably going to book out within the next couple of days,' he improvised. Lame, he knew, but he couldn't think of anything else to say on the spur of the moment.

'No problem, Mr Golding,' the manager assured him. 'Just call down to Reception on the morning of departure and they will have your bill waiting for you when you come down.'

'Thanks.' Max nodded with a dismissive smile.

'Sorry to hear that,' John murmured once the manager had left. 'In this job I very rarely get to meet the same people two nights in a row, let alone for a whole week,' he explained ruefully.

Max grimaced, knowing that his own job wasn't much better. Apart from Jude and a couple of other regular employees, he rarely saw the same person twice either; the Calendar sisters, because of their reluctance to sell, were the exception rather than the rule.

'So what's the real story on Meridew's hand?' he prompted lightly.

'Well—' John gave a knowing grin '—he says he sprained it putting in some cupboards at home, but we all think that Mrs Meridew either hit him or threw something at him!'

Max raised dark brows. 'There's a *Mrs* Meridew?'

'Oh, yes,' the barman confirmed with feeling. 'He wheels her out regularly every year for the staff Christmas party, and a more formidable woman you wouldn't hope to meet. She's twice the size of Meridew, obviously wears the trousers at home—which is probably why he's such a tartar when he's here!' he concluded heavily.

Under any other circumstances, Max would have found the other man's description of Peter Meridew's married life amusing, to say the least. But in this case…

Josh said he had recognized the voice of the man that had attacked him, although he couldn't remember where he remembered it from. Peter Meridew had an obviously soft spot for January. He had been in the room when Josh had kissed her. He had been walking around like a bear with a sore head all week. He also had a suspect injury to his hand. And a formidable wife who probably made his life miserable at home.

Still circumstantial, but surely worth investigating further?

'I have to go and make a telephone call,' he told John before swallowing down the last of his whisky. 'Enjoy the rest of the evening,' he added derisively.

'Not much chance of that!' John grimaced.

Max gave him a sympathetic smile before leaving the bar to go up to his hotel suite. There were still a few bits of information he needed before even attempting to talk to the police, but if his suspicion was correct...!

May was the one to answer the telephone at the Calendar farm, her businesslike tone easily discernible from January's husky voice and the derisive March.

'Hi, May, it's Max,' he told her abruptly. 'Could I speak to January?'

'She isn't here,' May told him with what sounded like a certain amount of satisfaction in her voice.

Max frowned his irritation. 'Where is she?'

'Max—'

'I need to know, May,' he told her determinedly.

'Why?' she prompted suspiciously.

Because he thought January might be at the centre of this latest attack. Because he suspected the manager of the hotel as being the attacker. Because he needed to know where January was now so that he could ensure that she was in no danger!

But he couldn't tell May any of those things without alarming her, possibly unnecessarily!

'I just heard her car outside,' May told him irritably. 'If you'll just hang on a minute...'

Max waited on the end of the line for what seemed much longer than a minute, and as the seconds ticked by he began to wonder if January had refused to speak to him. Not that he could blame her; they hadn't exactly parted on friendly terms earlier!

'Yes?' January finally came on the line to question cautiously.

Max felt a surge of relief just at the sound of her voice. Although, with Peter Meridew still on duty at the hotel, his worries concerning January's safety had probably been groundless.

'Where have you been?' With the suspicions of the last few minutes, his tone was sharper than he intended. 'I thought you were going straight home.' He forced lightness into his tone.

'Not that it's any of your business, but I called in to see Sara,' she explained stiffly.

'How is she?' he prompted huskily.

'As you would expect, very upset,' January came back sharply.

Not half as upset as January was going to be if his fears should turn out to be correct!

'Max, why did you telephone me?' she asked impatiently.

He sighed, knowing from her tone that she was annoyed with him, probably because of his own abruptness earlier this evening. 'I just wanted to ask you a question, January,' he told her briskly.

'Max—'

'Just one question, January,' he insisted firmly at her obvious impatience, 'then I won't bother you again.' Tonight, at least…!

She took a long time answering. 'Okay,' she finally agreed warily. 'One question.'

'How long have you been working at the hotel?'

'How long—? Max!' she murmured frustratedly. 'What on earth does that have to do with anything?'

A great deal, if his suspicions were correct. But he wasn't about to alarm her by telling her any of that.

'I would just like to know,' he came back evasively.

January gave an impatient sigh. 'About seven months, I think,' she told him irritatedly. 'Yes, it would be seven months,' she confirmed. 'I started some time in May. But what—?'

'That's all I wanted to know,' he cut in briskly, his thoughts racing.

Seven months. Seven attacks. What had seemed like an outrageous suspicion on his part now took on a much more sinister turn.

'Max—'

'I promised it would only be the one question, January,' he told her brightly. 'Enjoy what's left of the evening!' He rang off before she could question him any further.

As no doubt she had wanted to do! But there was no way he could confide in January concerning the suspicions he now had about Peter Meridew. That would only alarm and distress her.

Which left him in a position of wondering what to do now!

Of course he could just be overreacting. Could be reading things into situations that simply weren't there. After all, it had been six women who were attacked previously; only Josh was the exception.

Could Max seriously go to the police with his suspicions, or should he just bide his time a bit longer? Even if time wasn't something he had a whole lot of!

One thing he knew for certain, any thoughts he might have had about returning to America in the near future were now put on indefinite hold; he had no intention of going anywhere until this situation was well and truly sorted out!

Until he knew that January was safe…

CHAPTER ELEVEN

'STILL here?' January greeted Max rudely when she arrived at work on Thursday evening and found him once again sitting at the bar. 'Don't you have any little old ladies to throw out of their homes into the snow?' she added challengingly. 'Evening, John,' she greeted more warmly as she walked over to the piano.

Her mood had alternated between annoyance and puzzlement since Max's telephone call yesterday evening, the former usually winning out, her resentment at his wanting to know where she had been far outweighing any puzzlement she might feel concerning the strange unrelatedness of that single question he had asked her.

'And a good evening to you, too, January,' Max drawled as he turned on his bar stool to watch her. 'And, unless I'm mistaken, there isn't any snow left for me to throw the little old ladies onto; it's all melted away!'

'Your boss intends turning Hanworth Manor into a hotel and health club!' she returned scathingly, March at last having come with the information they wanted. 'This is Yorkshire, Max, not the south of France!'

His brows rose over mocking blue eyes. 'You don't think the people of Yorkshire are into health and beauty?'

'On the contrary, I'm sure that they are,' she snapped. 'I just don't think your boss has studied the climate in this area too well. The snow a couple of days ago is typical for this time of year!'

A hotel and health club, with luxury accommodation, as well as a gym and indoor swimming pool, the pièce de résistance an eighteen-hole golf course—of which, according to March's information on the preliminary proposal, their farm stood smack in the middle!

Max shook his head. 'This is all just speculation on your part, January—'

'Actually, it isn't,' she told him with satisfaction; March's information came 'from the horse's mouth', so to speak. Not that she intended telling Max that—he and, from the little she already knew of him, Jude Marshall were not men to let the situation rest there if they were to find out someone was leaking information concerning the plans for Hanworth Manor. 'You're going to meet quite a lot of local opposition to the idea, you know,' she added challengingly.

Although she wasn't too sure that would actually be the case…

Unemployment here was quite high, and the health and country club promised employment for quite a lot of people in the area. Although that was something else she didn't intend telling Max!

'Headed by the Calendar sisters, no doubt,' Max drawled wryly.

'No doubt,' she echoed tauntingly. 'Somehow I don't think our cows and sheep will welcome the idea of having golf balls whistling past their ears as they try to graze!'

Max's gaze narrowed warningly. 'Perhaps we should talk about this some other time—'

'Yes, we could always talk about the strangeness of

your telephone call last night, instead!' she cut in, once again challenging.

His expression became grim as he stood up to walk over to her. 'I would really rather you didn't inform the whole world of our private conversations,' he muttered harshly, glancing around them pointedly.

There were three other people in the bar beside themselves, John behind the bar, and a couple sitting in the corner of the room, obviously having eyes—and ears!—for no one but each other as they talked softly together in between kisses. Hardly the 'whole world'!

January gave a dismissive shrug. 'Well?' she prompted softly, dark brows raised enquiringly. 'Of what possible interest can it be to you when I started working here?'

'I was curious, that's all.' He shrugged.

January's frown turned to one of perplexity. 'You were curious?'

'Yes,' he dismissed abruptly. 'Shouldn't you have started singing by now?' he prompted. 'John tells me that Peter Meridew is in a foul mood this week.'

She had seen that for herself when she'd walked through Reception earlier and the manager had looked pointedly at his watch because she'd been five minutes late in arriving!

She shot Max a dismissive glance. 'Perhaps you should spend a little less time talking to the hotel staff and get on with the business you're paid for!'

His mouth quirked into a smile. 'The Calendar sisters are my business at the moment, and as you're one of them…'

In other words, he wasn't going anywhere, had every intention of staying here for the whole evening.

Great!

But as the bar steadily filled up, most people seeming to welcome getting out for the evening after the recent snow, January was able to ignore Max for the main part. After all, she consoled herself, he couldn't hang around in Yorkshire for ever.

Just long enough to disturb and annoy her!

'I'll walk you out to your car,' he offered as she packed her things away at the end of the evening, the bar having slowly emptied.

Not after what happened last time!

'There's no need,' she refused lightly. 'John has already offered to go with me,' she added triumphantly.

'Unless you would rather go with Mr Golding,' John put in awkwardly, having shut the bar up. 'I just thought, after what happened on Monday evening…' He gave a shrug.

'That's fine,' Max told the other man warmly. 'You see, January, I'm not the only one who thinks you should take more care!'

If he was annoyed at being usurped in this way, then he certainly wasn't showing it, January thought disgruntedly. And then realized how ridiculous she was being. She had deliberately accepted John's offer earlier for the very reason she didn't want to be put in a position of having to accept one from Max—and now she was angry with him for not trying harder!

'I'm sure I would be perfectly all right on my own,' she told Max waspishly.

Max shrugged. 'Better safe than sorry.'

She raised her eyes heavenwards. 'It's too late at night for clichés!'

He chuckled softly before turning to the barman. 'Make sure you actually see her getting into her car and driving away, John; she has a habit of taking diversions!'

She gasped. 'You—'

'Goodnight, January.' Max bent down to kiss her lightly on the lips. 'I'll leave her in your capable hands, then, John,' he told the other man with obvious amusement.

She shot him a furious glare before striding from the bar, John endeavouring to keep up with her. Something he seemed to be having trouble doing as he favoured his left foot slightly.

'I twisted my ankle playing football at the weekend,' he explained with a grimace as January slowed down so that he could catch her up. 'It made me realize I'm getting too old for that lark!' he added disgustedly.

January had no idea how old the barman actually was; with his receding hairline, but boyish looks, he could be anywhere between twenty-five and forty.

'As long as you enjoy it.' She smiled, still completely aware of Max as he walked over to get in one of the lifts. 'I—'

'January…?'

She turned to find Peter Meridew walking purposefully towards her. Just what she needed at the end of an already stressful evening!

'If I could just talk to Miss Calendar alone…?' The manager's words and look gave John a pointed dismissal.

John gave her a rueful grimace. 'I'll see you tomorrow, then, January. Mr Meridew.' He nodded abruptly, leaving with obvious reluctance.

What had she done now? January wondered frustratedly. Okay, so she had been five minutes late arriving, but as the bar had been particularly busy this evening she had also carried on singing fifteen minutes over her usual time…

'Perhaps you would like to come through to my office?' Peter Meridew said firmly.

And perhaps she wouldn't! It was almost one-thirty in the morning, for goodness' sake—and she had a home to go to, even if this man preferred to stay out of his as much as possible; it was common knowledge amongst the hotel staff that Peter Meridew often stayed on working long after his shift should have ended because of the formidable wife waiting for him at home! Normally she felt quite sorry for his obviously unhappy home life, but at one-thirty in the morning she had to admit her sympathy was running a little thin!

'Couldn't this wait until tomorrow evening?' she suggested lightly.

His expression tightened. 'I received a visit from the police today in connection with the attacks being carried out in the area,' he bit out tersely, obviously not at all pleased at having police calling at his hotel, for any reason.

January frowned her confusion. 'What does that have to do with me?'

'On a personal level, nothing,' he accepted. 'However, they are suggesting we change our policy as regards ensuring the safety of certain employees.'

Somehow January didn't like the sound of this…! Besides the fact that it sounded extremely familiar…?

'Yes?' she prompted warily.

Peter Meridew gave a terse inclination of his head. 'I am afraid that, until such time as the attacker is found and incarcerated, we will have to dispense with your services.'

'What?' January gasped, not seeing the connection at all.

The manager's mouth thinned. 'Yes. Of course you may finish off the week,' he added hurriedly.

'That's very big of you,' January muttered, too tired—and angry!—to feel like being overly polite; besides, the man was effectively putting her out of a job at the end of the week!

'I'm really no happier about this than you are.' Peter Meridew sighed. 'We have been more than pleased with your work. But apparently one of the guests has complained that three evenings a week you regularly leave the hotel, alone, at a very late hour—'

'*One* of the guests…?' January cut in forcefully, turning to look at the lifts; as she had suspected Max had already gone up to his suite. But it didn't take her two guesses to know who 'the guest' was who had lodged the complaint.

Or to guess why he had done such a thing! He really was Jude Marshall's man, wasn't he, out to ruin the Calendar sisters if he couldn't get them out of the farm any other way? First put her out of a job, and then he would no doubt start on March. Well, that was what he thought!

She gave Peter Meridew a warm smile. 'I'm sure the police don't actually have the authority to instruct you to sack me?'

'I'm not sacking you, January.' The manager looked slightly flustered at the suggestion. 'But, after giving the situation due consideration, I am of the opinion it is the best way to deal with the problem. For the moment,' he added hastily. 'We don't, of course, want to lose your services indefinitely.'

No, she would just bet they didn't; she never demurred about staying longer than she was supposed to do, or coming in for special occasions if necessary, and the wages really weren't that good. Just necessary in order for them to be able to keep the farm. Which brought her right back to Max Golding…!

She forced herself to remain calm. 'Did they tell you which of the guests made the complaint?' she prompted interestedly.

'I did enquire, but… They were disinclined to tell me,' Peter Meridew snapped abruptly, obviously most displeased with this police reticence. 'However, I do accept that it is in the interest of your safety, and as such—'

'"You have to dispense with my services",' January finished for him tautly. 'And I have no say in the matter whatsoever?' she prompted disgustedly.

His expression softened. 'January—'

'It's okay, Peter,' she cut in impatiently, shaking her head. 'I fully accept the position you have been put in.' And who *had* put him—and her!—there! 'If you don't mind, I would like to leave now…?'

'Not at all,' he accepted, obviously relieved she hadn't made more of a scene about the situation. 'Perhaps I could escort you out to your car?' he offered.

January gave a decisive shake of her head. 'I just have to do something first—but thanks.'

If Max thought he was going to get away with this without protest from her, then he was in for a surprise—because she had every intention of going up to his suite right now and telling him exactly what she thought of him, and his machinations.

Concern for her safety, indeed!

In other circumstances, Max might have felt pleased to find January standing outside his hotel suite at one-thirty in the morning knocking to come in—but one glance at her obviously furious expression, grey eyes blazing, two angry spots of colour on her cheeks in an otherwise white face, was enough to tell him this was not a social call!

'Would you like to come—? Ah, you would,' he murmured derisively as she pushed past him into the suite, closing the door softly behind her before following her back into the room, glad now that he had stopped to check his e-mails rather than going straight to bed; something was obviously seriously wrong. Which meant something must have happened since they'd parted fifteen minutes ago; January hadn't been too enamoured of him then, but she was furiously angry now!

'Drink?' he offered hopefully.

'No,' she refused tautly. 'But you go ahead—with any luck it might choke you!'

'Hmm, in that case, I think I'll pass, too,' he drawled warily.

What could have happened in the fifteen minutes since they'd parted? The last he had seen of January she had been on her way out the door, John at her side.

'Pity!' January snapped, giving him a scathing glance. 'I've just been having a cosy chat with Peter Meridew—'

'What?' Max's wariness turned to shock.

January hadn't left with John, after all?

Damn it, he should have waited until she was safely out to her car, Max remonstrated with himself, should have—

'You heard,' January bit out accusingly. 'You'll be pleased to know, he just sacked me!'

'He what?' To say it was the last thing Max had been expecting to hear would be an understatement!

'Max, as I really don't think there is anything wrong with your hearing,' January began scathingly, 'I have no intention of repeating everything I say! I'm allowed to stay on until the end of the week, but after that my services have been dispensed with. For the moment,' she added harshly. 'And we both know why, don't we?' She glared at him.

Max looked across at her frowningly, totally nonplussed. Peter Meridew had just told January that he didn't want her coming to the hotel after the weekend? In the circumstances, that didn't make any sense to Max whatsoever.

'Do we?' he delayed warily, his thoughts racing.

The anger deepened in those beautiful grey eyes—although Max wisely decided that now wasn't the time to tell January how beautiful she looked when she was angry!

He remembered Jude telling him he had once said that to one of the women in his life—and the next morning he had sported a bruise on his jaw to prove it!

'You won't succeed in getting us out of the farm like this, Max,' January told him scornfully. 'I'll just get myself another job—and then you'll be back where you started!'

She thought he had deliberately—!

His mouth tightened as his own anger started to rise. 'Now, listen here—'

'No—*you* listen,' she cut in forcefully. 'You may have managed to lose me my job, but all that's done is make me all the more determined that you won't succeed.'

'January—'

'Can you deny it was you who made the complaint to the police about my leaving here alone late at night?' she challenged, that small pointed chin raised defiantly. 'A complaint, because of these random attacks late at night, they took straight to Peter Meridew.'

Max winced at the accusation. He hadn't exactly complained to the police, more suggested, in the course of his conversation with them, that it probably wasn't a good idea for a woman to be travelling alone at that time of night. How could he possibly have known that idiot of a manager would turn round and sack January on the basis of that?

Added to which, if his suspicions were correct, the manager's subsequent actions made absolutely no sense to him…!

If they were correct…

And it certainly looked as if they might not be in the light of Peter Meridew's decision concerning January continuing to work here.

Unless it was some sort of attempt at misdirection on the other man's part? Although, for the life of him, Max couldn't think what that could possibly be!

He drew in a sharp breath. 'Look, I admit that during my conversation with the police, concerning that altercation with Josh at the weekend, I may have mentioned your late-night drives—'

'Oh, you ''admit'' to that, do you?' she flared scathingly. 'Well, I—'

'January, for goodness' sake, listen to me—'

'No!' she snapped forcefully, eyes blazing, her whole body tense with anger. '*You* listen to me!' she snapped even more vehemently. 'Stay out of my life, Max. Stay out of my sisters' lives. In fact, just stay completely away from all of us!' She was breathing hard in her agitation.

She had never looked lovelier to Max!

'January…!' he groaned, his hands moving up instinctively.

'Do not touch me!' She stepped back as if burnt.

Or as if his merest touch might contaminate her in some way!

It was altogether too much for Max, all his own earlier decisions to keep an emotional distance between himself and January evaporating like so much mist. He couldn't bear to have her look at him like that. He just couldn't!

He tried to take her in his arms, only to have his chest pummelled with clenched fists as she fought against him.

'Let-me-go-Max,' she told him through gritted teeth, pushing against his chest now in an effort to dislodge the steel of his arms.

'I can't,' he told her gruffly.

'Let me go, Max, or I'll—I'll—'

'You'll what?' He frowned.

She became suddenly still in his arms, her eyes filled with tears now as she looked up at him. 'I don't want this, Max,' she told him huskily. 'Don't you understand?' she choked, shaking her head.

Only too well! She couldn't wait to be out of his arms, to get away from him!

Max felt pain unlike any he had ever known before, knew that at that moment he would do or say anything to erase that look of loathing—for him!—from her face.

He drew in a harsh breath. 'It's you that doesn't understand,' he rasped. 'I did those things, told the police about your lone drives home late at night, for one reason and one reason only—'

'And we both know what that is, don't we?' she flashed with some of her earlier spirit.

'I did it because I *care*, January!' he bit out tautly, his hands moving to grasp her upper arms as he shook her slightly. 'Because I care!' he repeated harshly.

She shook her head disbelievingly. 'There's only one thing you care about, Max—and that's yourself!' she returned scornfully.

Maybe that had been true once. Maybe it still was, in some ways. But not in the way she meant.

He shook her again. 'You stubborn, pigheaded—'

'Yes, I'm stubborn and pigheaded,' she confirmed self-derisively. 'But I would much rather be that way than cold and heartless—like you!'

Max became suddenly still, his hands falling back to his sides as he stepped away from her, his gaze guarded now as he held his inner emotions firmly in check. 'Is that really what you think of me?' he finally murmured evenly.

January's mouth twisted humourlessly. 'What else?' she sneered. 'But isn't that what you wanted?' she challenged scornfully. 'Of course it is! After all, you're Max Golding, legal henchman of Jude Marshall—and neither of you makes any secret of the fact that you take no prisoners!'

Was that what he had become? Not as far as he was aware. It certainly wasn't what he had set out to be fifteen years ago…

But was that really what he had become? Somehow that wasn't a palatable thought.

'I've said all I came here to say,' January told him dismissively as he made no further comment, picking up her bag from where she had thrown it down on the table earlier. 'But I meant it about staying away from me and my family in the future,' she added warningly.

Max could see that she did, could see the cold anger in her eyes, the scorn for him that she made no effort to hide.

The pain deepened inside him, so much so that it held him immobile as he watched January walk away from him, the door closing softly behind her as she left.

Max knew she hadn't just walked out of the hotel suite, but out of his life.

For ever.

Never before, not once in all of his thirty-seven years, had he told anyone that he cared about them. And he cared more about January than he ever had anyone before.

More than cared, if he was honest. With himself, at least.

And, after the things she had just said, he knew she felt nothing but loathing for him in return...!

CHAPTER TWELVE

SOMEONE was following her!

January wasn't quite sure when she first became aware of the car following some distance behind hers, but she had been sure of it for at least the last three miles, every turn she took down increasingly country roads—deserted roads!—the car behind making the same turn seconds later.

Suddenly Max's scathing comments about the safety of her driving home alone late at night no longer seemed quite so ridiculous!

Unless it was Max himself who was following her…?

Surely not; she knew he was a determined man, but surely not a vindictive one? And it was more than vindictive to scare her in this way!

Then who was it?

She gave another glance in the driving mirror, those two headlights still there, if some distance away, too far back for her to even begin to identify the make of the car, let alone identify the driver. But she certainly didn't intend stopping the car in order to confront the other driver, either!

But she didn't like this, didn't like it one little bit.

Of course, she could be wrong about the other car deliberately following her, it could just be someone else returning home late at night who also happened to live in her area. She could just be overreacting to this because of Max's dire warnings!

There was one way of testing that theory, January realized as she took note of where she had got to in the journey; in about half a mile or so there was a narrow lane that led onto the track that eventually reached the farm. And only their farm. If the person behind her took that same short cut then she was definitely being followed.

January's hands tightened on the steering wheel as the car followed on behind her as she turned down the lane, feeling hot and cold at the same time as she accepted she was definitely being followed.

To say she was alarmed now would be an understatement; she had never been so scared in her life!

The mobile telephone!

They had one mobile telephone between the three of them, May keeping it with her during the day as she worked about the farm, but insisting that January take it with her on the evenings she worked. She had always dismissed the necessity of it in the past, but at this particular moment she was glad of May's overprotectiveness!

But who did she call?

Her sisters at the farm?

Both May and March were heavy sleepers, and with the mobile here with her, the only other telephone was downstairs in the hallway.

Max?

Absolutely not!

The police, to tell them she thought she was being followed?

If she turned out to be wrong about that, she was going to end up looking extremely foolish.

But what if she wasn't wrong...?

The police, then, she decided hurriedly as the car behind followed her doggedly down the narrow lane—

No—wait a minute! The car had stopped, the headlights starting to fade away now as January took the turning up the track that led directly to the farm, able to heave a deep sigh of relief seconds later as she saw the vehicle was being turned around before driving back in the direction they had just come.

How strange. How very, very odd.

Strange and odd it might be, but January was shaking badly with reaction by the time she parked the car in the farmyard ten minutes later and climbed out onto the cobbles!

Perhaps it was as well, after all, that after tomorrow she would no longer have that long drive back from the hotel at night; she had the evening off anyway on Saturday, to attend Sara and Josh's wedding.

Although she had no intention of ever giving Max the satisfaction of knowing he might have been right about these late-night drives, still maintained that he had no right to interfere in her life in the high-handed way that he had.

She had no intention of telling her sisters about the car following her home tonight, either; they had enough worries already. With only one evening left to work, it wasn't worth mentioning.

'I don't understand.' May frowned the following morning as the two of them sat drinking coffee together, March having already left for work. 'What reason did Peter Meridew give for letting you go?'

'Sacking me,' January corrected dryly. 'My own safety, apparently.' She grimaced. 'A likely story!' she added disgustedly, knowing exactly who was responsible for her jobless state after this evening. And why!

'But don't worry, I'll get another job,' she assured optimistically.

Quite where, she wasn't sure. She could always wait for the health and country club to open and apply for a job there—she didn't think!

May still frowned. 'Perhaps, in the circumstances, we really should consider Jude Marshall's offer to buy the farm...'

'What?' January sat up stiffly, staring at her sister incredulously. May couldn't be serious, not after all they had already gone through! 'I will get another job, May,' she assured her determinedly. 'Besides, if we sold the farm, where would we all live?' She frowned.

May shrugged. 'March could get a flat in town, which would save her all the travelling to and fro to work. The two of you could probably get a flat together,' she reasoned.

January couldn't believe she was hearing this! 'And what about you?'

'Me?' Her sister looked a little uncomfortable now. 'Well, the thing is, January— Well, you see— I—'

'What is it?' January prompted warily; May was the least tongue-tied person she had ever known.

May's cheeks coloured. 'I've had this offer, you see—Well, not exactly an offer—more like—'

'May!' January protested impatiently. 'Just spit it out, will you?'

If her sister had a boyfriend, someone May was serious about, then it was the first January had heard of it. But if that were the case... The three of them had always known that they could only continue to run the farm if all three of them were in agreement, if it was what they all three wanted to go on doing. One of them wanting to marry would certainly change that. Even if the man agreed to live on the farm, there was no way he would want the other two sisters living with them, too. As she had learnt only too well from her brief relationship with Ben!

May gave an embarrassed sigh. 'Someone approached me, after I did the pantomime at Christmas, suggested that I go for a screen test, that—well, that—'

'May…!' January said excitedly. 'Really?'

May flushed uncomfortably. 'I wasn't completely honest about going to the dentist the other day, I actually had lunch with this director. He—' She moistened dry lips. 'Apparently he spent Christmas with his sister's family nearby, came to the pantomime with them all, and saw me—January, if I go for the test, and it's successful, he wants me to appear in a film he's going to begin making this summer!' she finished incredulously.

January had known her sister was good, very good in fact, but this—!

It was beyond any of their wildest dreams. Beyond May's, she was sure.

'But don't you see?' May wailed. 'If I have the screen test, and if this director offers me the part, I would no longer be here to work on the farm,' she pointed out emotionally. 'You and March simply wouldn't be able to cope here on your own, job or no job.'

January could see only too well. But, at the same time, this was too good an opportunity for May to turn down.

'But of course you must do it,' she told May decisively. 'May, you didn't say no?' She groaned as her sister still looked unconvinced.

'I said—maybe.' May grimaced. 'I needed time to

think about it,' she defended at January's reproachful look. 'After all, it's a big step.'

'But if you're successful—!'

'I'm not sure I want to be successful. Not in that way,' May added hardly.

'But you have been thinking about it?' January persisted.

'Yes,' her sister sighed. 'And now that you've lost your job, and we have an offer on the farm, anyway… It all seems to be leading to one thing. Maybe this is what we're supposed to do. I don't know, January. I just don't know.' She gave a weary shake of her head.

January knew that she would personally hate having to tell Max that they had changed their mind about accepting Jude Marshall's offer, would hate even more the look of triumph that would be on his face once he had been told. But, at the same time, May deserved her chance at success, didn't she…?

'Let's see what March thinks about it all, hmm?' January prompted, although she was pretty sure March would be of the same mind as herself.

As sisters they had always looked out for each other, but May had always been the mainstay of the family, the one who took the most responsibility; it was only fair that she be given the chance to do something totally for herself.

Having Max arrive at the farm later that afternoon, to inform them that he was returning to America in the morning, along with a recommendation to Jude Marshall that he work his plans for the health and country club around the Calendar farm, was not something either she or May could have envisaged!

But he was intelligent enough to realize that neither January nor May was exactly thrilled by the news, looking at them both with narrowed eyes as the three of them stood in the warm kitchen. 'That was what you wanted, wasn't it?' he rasped.

'It was, yes,' May was the one to answer guardedly.

'January?' Max bit out tautly, blue gaze compelling.

She met that gaze reluctantly, very aware of how disturbingly attractive he looked in the dark business suit and white shirt he was wearing today. Even more aware of the things she had said to him the previous evening—and the huge backdown they were probably about to make.

But it was for May, wasn't it…?

'It was what we wanted, yes,' she confirmed slowly.

His gaze narrowed. 'But you have since changed your mind?' he guessed shrewdly.

January looked pleadingly at May, knowing she couldn't do this. She just couldn't!

'We're—thinking about it, yes,' her sister told Max dismissively.

Max looked at the two of them disbelievingly, shaking his head, obviously completely baffled by this seeming about-face on their part.

As well he might be, January acknowledged with an inward wince.

Women, would he ever understand them? Max wondered dazedly as he looked at January and May.

He hadn't slept at all the previous night, had gone over and over in his mind the things January had said to him, punishing himself for his own determination never to let anyone into his life, never to care about anyone enough for them to be able to hurt him.

Because January had hurt him the night before. Had hurt him more than he had ever been hurt before.

Finally, he had known that the only thing left for him to do was to go back to America, to explain the situation to Jude, and let him take over from there, if he cared to. One thing Max was very sure of: he couldn't do this any more…

And now, it seemed, the Calendar sisters had changed their mind about selling, after all!

Without being invited to do so—he would probably wait all day if he expected any politeness from January!—he sat down abruptly in one of the kitchen chairs. 'Would someone mind telling me what is going on?' he prompted wearily—and not only from lack of sleep.

'Here, have some coffee.' May poured some from the pot into a mug and placed it in front of him.

A double whisky would probably have been more beneficial, Max decided with a grimace, but sipped the hot coffee anyway. 'Well?' he finally prompted when neither sister seemed inclined to add anything.

'I only said we're thinking about it, Max,' May reminded impatiently. 'Circumstances have changed—'

'So January informed me, only too volubly, last night!' He nodded tersely.

May shot January a sharply questioning look, January answering with a warning shake of her head.

'January being temporarily out of a job wasn't the circumstances you were talking about,' Max realized slowly, gaze narrowing speculatively. 'Care to tell me about it?' he prompted lightly.

'No!' January snapped.

'Yes,' May countered firmly, giving January a frown. 'You don't shoot the envoy, January,' she reproved teasingly.

Max's mouth twisted. 'I would like to stick around and watch one of you shoot Jude!'

'Be my guest,' January returned sharply. 'But, of course, you're going back to America, aren't you?' she added scathingly.

What he would most like to do at the moment was put her over his knee and give her a good spanking. A thought May, if the teasing smile she gave him was anything to go by, was all too aware of!

Going back to America was not the ideal thing for him to do with this attacker called the Night Striker still on the loose, but with January hating him in the way that she did, he didn't feel he could stay here, either.

To say he was disappointed in this uncertainty of the sisters about selling the farm after all would be an understatement. He had come to admire all three sisters for their determination this last week, had to admit he had half relished going back to Jude and telling him the answer was a definite no!

No doubt about it, he would never understand women. But this possible change of mind by the Calendar sisters ultimately made no difference to his own plans. Someone else could sort out the details, he really had had enough.

'I am,' he confirmed evenly. 'So what happened?' He turned to May—deciding, of the two, she was probably the one who would give him a straight answer. 'Is one of you getting married or something?' If it was January—!

He felt a jolt in his chest just at the thought of her marrying some faceless man. Just as well he was leaving!

'Or something,' May told him dryly.

Immediately starting Max's heart beating again. Until that moment he hadn't even been aware that it had stopped!

May looked slightly abashed. 'A director has approached me about appearing in a film he's going to make in the summer.' The words came out in a self-conscious rush. 'I'll probably be awful at it, but…' She gave a rueful shrug.

Aha! The answer to May's nonexistent dental appointment earlier in the week? The derisive smile May shot his way told him that his supposition was correct.

Well, well, well. So May might be going off for some time filming. And he already knew that March had a full-time job. So what was January going to do?

As if aware of his curiosity, January snapped, 'I've always wondered what it would be like to be part of the entertainment team on a cruise ship.'

'You have?' May frowned—obviously hearing this for the first time.

'I have,' January confirmed with an awkward shrug, at the same time shooting Max a resentful glare—obviously not at all happy with having him here as part of this family 'baring-of-hearts'.

A sentiment that he wholeheartedly agreed with—although, as January didn't think he had a heart, she probably wouldn't believe that!

He stood up abruptly, once again keeping his gaze firmly fixed on May. 'It all sounds great.' He nodded. 'I hope it works out for you. I just felt I owed it to you all to come and tell you what I plan on doing tomorrow.' He drew in a sharp breath; now that the time had actually come for him to part from January his legs felt like lead, his heart even heavier.

'That was very kind of you, Max,' May told him warmly. 'Wasn't it, January?' she prompted pointedly.

'Very,' she echoed dryly.

He gave a self-derisive smile. 'What she really means, May, is she'll be glad to see me go!' he murmured softly.

January gave him a level stare. 'Is that so surprising? You've done nothing but cause mayhem and confusion since you arrived here!' she accused, her anger obviously starting to rise, two spots of colour in the paleness of her cheeks too now.

'January!' May gasped.

'But he has, May,' she defended impatiently. 'He's harassed us about selling the farm,' she claimed heatedly—a little unfairly, Max thought. 'He's lost me my job, he claims because of concern over my safety,' she continued disgustedly. 'And now he's got me into such a state of paranoia that I've even started *imagining* people are following me home at night!'

Max tensed, his gaze narrowing with sudden alertness. 'Someone followed you home last night?' he echoed slowly.

'Of course not,' she dismissed irritably. 'I just thought they did—'

'Why did you think they did?' he cut in softly, every muscle and sinew of his body tensed now, a nerve pulsing in his cheek.

January gave a dismissive smile. 'Because they obviously live somewhere in the area and were driving home at the same time I was!' she snorted self-derisively.

Max looked at her searchingly. 'Are you sure?'

She nodded. 'I'm still here, aren't I?' she scorned.

Yes, she was—and as verbally resentful as ever. Oh,

well, what had he expected? Nothing had happened to change that since they'd parted last night. In fact, from what she had just said, the opposite!

'So you are,' he conceded dryly. 'But I understand you will be at the hotel this evening?' There was a notice up outside the piano-bar that tonight would be January's last performance for a while.

Max's mouth had thinned disapprovingly as he'd read the notice earlier; Peter Meridew obviously couldn't even do that right! By making such a public announcement the other man was effectively letting anyone who cared to know that January would be driving home alone this evening one last time...!

'Yes, I will,' January confirmed abruptly, her chin raised challengingly. 'Can I expect to see you there?'

His mouth twisted humourlessly. 'I wouldn't be surprised,' he drawled.

Her eyes flashed dark grey. 'Neither would I!'

He gave an acknowledging bow before turning to a frowning May; obviously she wasn't at all happy about her youngest sister's rudeness. 'I wish you every success with your possible acting career,' he told her warmly.

May looked embarrassed again. 'I haven't definitely decided to go ahead with that yet.'

'But she will,' January said determinedly.

'Maybe,' May conceded. 'Have a good flight home tomorrow, Max.'

Once again one of the sisters had assumed that his home was in America. But this time he was too weary to correct the mistake.

'Thanks,' he accepted with a smile. 'I'll see you later, then, January.'

She gave him a look that clearly said, Not if I see you first!

Max chuckled softly. 'Or perhaps not,' he allowed ruefully.

Although that humour faded as soon as he was outside, taking a moment to stand and look at the surrounding countryside with narrowed eyes.

Had someone followed January home last night? Or was it as she said, just another local resident driving home late at night?

He didn't know. And neither did she. Not really. She couldn't.

January wasn't going to like it, he knew, but this was definitely something the police should be made aware of.

He also had one more call to make this afternoon on his way back to the hotel to pack.

To Josh.

January might see all of this as some sort of paranoia on his part, but if it stopped her from getting hurt, paranoid was exactly what he would be!

CHAPTER THIRTEEN

'NO JOHN this evening?'

January turned to find Max just entering the bar, his opening comment drawing attention to the fact that there was someone else working behind the bar this evening.

Before his gaze narrowed on January's own appearance, a shutter coming down over those blue eyes as he took in the scarlet knee-length dress she was wearing this evening.

January's chin rose defensively as Max's gaze swept over her from head to toe; she had decided that if this really was her last evening working here, then she was going out with a flourish! The figure-hugging, scoop-necked scarlet dress was the result of that bravado.

She shrugged, determined to ignore Max's all-seeing gaze. 'He was here earlier, apparently, but has since gone off sick,' she answered Max's earlier comment. 'Probably still having trouble with his ankle,' she dismissed, a little disappointed that she wouldn't see John again before leaving; he had always been very kind to her. 'Football,' she explained at Max's frowning look.

His brow cleared, his smile derisive. 'I've never really understood this fascination with what has become England's national sport.'

'It isn't as boring as cricket?' January returned dryly.

Max chuckled softly. 'You could have a point there!'

Max looked more like a rugby player himself, his physique muscular to say the least, January allowed grudgingly.

Not that it was of any of her business, she told herself sharply; there was nothing more she needed to know about Max Golding. It was bad enough that she was in love with him!

'If you'll excuse me,' she said sharply, as usual feeling disturbed just by Max's presence in the same room as her, 'I have to get to work.'

He nodded. 'I have a few things to attend to myself,' he told her enigmatically. 'Perhaps I'll catch up with you later,' he added dismissively.

January watched him leave beneath lowered lashes. Tomorrow he would be gone. From the hotel. From England. From her life. How her heart ached just at the thought of it!

Only a few more hours to get through, she told herself determinedly. And then she could give in to the heartbreak that had been threatening since he'd come to the farm earlier to inform them he was leaving, going back to America.

Perhaps it was as well she would no longer be working here after tonight; she simply wouldn't have been able to come to the hotel without imagining Max here, her loss all the more acute because he really wasn't.

As she was aware of his absence during the early part of the evening. Strange how quickly she had become accustomed to his being here the evenings she worked, how flat the evening seemed because he wasn't there watching her with that intense blue gaze.

She had to stop this, she decided as she stood at the bar sipping sparkling water during her first break. Max had never really been in her life, so how could she feel so devastated now that he was going out of it? She didn't know—she just did!

How could she bear it?

How was she going to survive without his annoying—wonderful!—presence in her life?

'Penny for them?'

She turned sharply at the huskily intimate sound of his voice, hurriedly blinking back the tears that had blurred her vision. 'Shouldn't that be "cent"?' she came back lamely.

Max shook his head, frowning slightly. 'How many more times? I don't actually live in America, January.'

Her eyes widened. 'You don't?'

He gave another shake of his head. 'I have no idea why you thought that I did.'

'Because you said you had flown here from there.' She frowned. 'And Jude Marshall is there. I just assumed—' Somehow the thought that Max might actually still be in England somewhere, and not all the way across the Atlantic, made their parting not quite so hard to bear.

'I have an apartment in London, January,' he told her softly, his gaze searching now on the paleness of her face. 'An apartment I have a feeling I will be using a lot more in the near future,' he added dryly.

She looked at him quizzically. 'You will?'

'Yes,' he confirmed with satisfaction. 'January—'

'Mr Golding?'

They both turned at the sound of that enquiring voice, January's gaze widening even further as she took in the police uniform the man was wearing. What on earth—?

'Yes?' Max answered sharply, January actually able to feel his sudden tension.

The policeman glanced at January. 'If you could just step outside for a few minutes, sir,' he prompted quietly.

January was feeling tense herself now. What on earth

could the police want with Max? Surely they didn't think—?

'I'm coming with you,' she told Max determinedly as he turned to leave with the other man.

He glanced back at her, blue gaze guarded now. 'I would much rather you didn't,' he said softly.

'Too bad,' she snapped forcefully, moving quickly to his side, her hand moving to rest lightly in his crooked arm.

Max looked down at her questioningly. 'I'm not about to be arrested, January,' he teased huskily.

She wasn't so sure about that! And if that were the case, and it had anything to do with the attacks over the last seven months, she had every intention of telling the police exactly how ridiculous they were being; Max hadn't even been in England when most of those attacks had occurred!

'You would be Miss Calendar?' The policeman frowned as he became aware of her presence. 'Miss January Calendar?'

Her hand tightened on Max's arm. 'I would,' she confirmed warily.

'Don't look so worried, January.' Max bent his head to tell her soothingly. 'They aren't about to arrest you, either!'

'I should think not,' she bristled indignantly.

'However…' Even as Max began to speak the door to Peter Meridew's office opened, several people emerging, obviously also policemen, a couple in plain clothes, two others in uniform restraining another man between the two of them as he struggled and shouted abuse.

'John…!' January gasped, before looking up disbelievingly at Max.

His expression was grim, his hand tight on hers as

it rested on his arm. 'John is the one who has been carrying out the attacks,' he told her gently.

'John is—?' She shook her head dazedly before turning back to look at John.

A John who looked totally unlike the likeable man she had come to know over the last few months, his face twisted into an ugly mask as he continued to shout and struggle as he was taken from the hotel.

John…!

He was the attacker? The man who had attacked six women? Who had beaten Josh so badly on Monday evening? The man who—

The man who had attacked Josh on Monday evening…

She looked up sharply at Max as a terrible truth began to grow inside her, seeing the confirmation of her suspicions in Max's grimly set features—before blackness washed over her and she began to fall.

Max looked down worriedly at January as she lay on the sofa in Peter Meridew's office. Her face was so pale, dark shadows beneath her eyes, her breathing shallow.

He had managed to catch her before she'd actually hit the tiled floor, picking her up to carry her through to the manager's office, dismissing the other man from his own office with an imperious wave of his hand, in one way relieved that January had been spared the next few minutes of dealing with the police, but in another way concerned about what to say to her when she did regain consciousness. Because he had seen the truth in her eyes seconds before she'd collapsed, knew then that she had realized exactly why John had carried out those attacks.

Knew that she was the catalyst…

'It was me, wasn't it?' January murmured beside him, as if the intensity of Max's thoughts had penetrated her unconsciousness.

Max turned to her sharply. 'How do you feel?' he prompted concernedly, taking one of her hands in his, dismayed at how cold she felt despite the warmth in the hotel.

She blinked, tears sparkling against her long lashes. 'John did those things because of some sort of misguided—feelings, for me, didn't he?' she repeated brokenly.

Max's hand tightened on hers. 'It wasn't your fault, January,' he told her firmly. 'You must never think that. The man was obsessed.' He shook his head grimly. 'I never realized before today how normal an insane person can appear!'

She gave the ghost of a smile. 'I'm not sure that remark was exactly complimentary to me...?'

Good, she was getting her sense of humour back; it was a start.

Max gave her a reassuring smile. 'It was meant to be, I can assure you. Are you feeling better?' he asked as she swung her legs to the floor and sat up next to him on the sofa.

She didn't look better, her face still deathly pale, those tears still trembling against her lashes.

'January, you couldn't have known,' he told her intensely. 'Damn it, until I spoke to Josh this afternoon I thought it was Peter Meridew!' he added self-derisively—and instantly wished he hadn't as January's face paled even more. 'It was mentioning that to Josh this afternoon that jogged his memory into realizing it was the *hotel barman's* voice he had recognized. The police have been watching John since this afternoon,' he added grimly.

'You knew?' January gasped. 'You really did know?'

Max gave a pained frown as her voice broke emotionally. 'The attack on Josh set off alarm bells in my head.' He nodded. 'Especially when he told us he had recognized the voice of his attacker. I just came to the wrong conclusion, that's all.' He grimaced. 'Maybe I can be forgiven for that. Peter Meridew was in the room when Josh kissed you on Saturday evening, and he also seemed to be around a lot whenever you were in the piano bar. But then so was John,' he acknowledged hardly.

January still looked totally dazed. 'But if—if John, felt that he had some sort of—of claim on me, why didn't he attack you, too?'

Max gave a rueful smile. 'Good question. I've been wondering that myself.' He grimaced. 'Maybe he just didn't think I was going to be around long enough to be a problem. Whereas Josh and Peter Meridew…' He broke off pointedly.

January shook her head. 'Why did he attack those other women?'

'Because it seems that, at one time or another, he felt they had scorned or rejected him. Who really knows the workings of a disturbed mind?' he rasped harshly.

January swallowed hard. 'Maybe the same thing would have happened to me if I had ever been less than friendly towards him.' She shuddered just at the thought of it.

Max's hand tightened about hers. 'You mustn't think that way, January,' he told her forcefully. 'John has been arrested. He's no longer a danger to anyone—thank goodness. He completely lost it when he came in to work this evening and discovered you were no longer going to be working here, instantly knew who was responsible. The police caught him in the act of attacking Peter Meridew. I don't know if you heard him just now—' Max grimaced '—but he's already said enough for the police to charge him with all the attacks,' he explained softly, all the time watching January concernedly.

She swallowed hard. 'Do you think it was John that followed me home last night?'

'Ah. No.' Max grimaced self-consciously. 'I checked on that earlier. It was actually a police car. Apparently, they had thought they were following at a safe distance, but my constant warnings had obviously put you on a bigger state of alertness than we thought. I'm sorry for alarming you in that way, January,' he added as she looked more pale than ever.

This must all have come as such a shock to her. After all, he had had several hours to come to terms with the idea himself, and he still found the whole thing highly disturbing. January had known John a lot longer than he had, had obviously liked the man. Only to find out he wasn't at all what she had thought he was.

Perhaps he would be able to persuade her that *he* wasn't what she had thought he was either…?

One thing Max knew for certain, whatever his plans might have been before tonight, he no longer intended going back to America.

He couldn't bear the thought of going anywhere if January wouldn't go with him!

CHAPTER FOURTEEN

JANUARY felt ill, had never felt so sick in her life. John. Nice, friendly, *invisible* John. Who ever would have thought of it?

Max had thought of it!

Okay, so he had initially suspected the wrong man, but he had ultimately been perfectly correct in warning her to take care. And all she had done was to give him a hard time over what she had considered his interference!

God, all those times she had talked with John, shared a joke or two with him, accepted his offer to walk her out to her car—!

She repressed a shudder, looked frowningly at Max. 'I owe you an apology—' She broke off as Max stood up abruptly, frowning up at him now.

'I don't want your apology, January,' he rasped, blue gaze blazing, hands clenched at his sides. 'Neither do I want your gratitude,' he added harshly.

She flinched at the force of his emotions. But was it so surprising that Max was angry with her? He had tried to help her, and she had blocked or mocked him at every turn.

She sighed. 'I appreciate you're angry—'

'Too right I'm angry!' he shot back forcefully. 'I should have looked after you better. Should have checked and double-checked on my suspicions, not just told the police about them—before deciding to run away!' he bit out self-disgustedly. 'Well, I'm not running any more, January,' he told her forcefully. 'I'm not going anywhere. Do I make myself clear?' He stood over her gloweringly.

January blinked a little dazedly at this sudden attack. She had meant *he* had a right to be angry with *her*, not himself. 'I don't understand.' She shook her head in puzzlement.

Max came down on his haunches beside her, his gaze intent on her face. 'I'm not going to America or anywhere else, January. In fact, in future I'm going to stick to you like glue,' he added grimly.

'But—but now that John has—now that he's been arrested, I'm not in any danger.' She still felt nauseous at how friendly she had been with a man who attacked seemingly at random. Although she was sure that someone would eventually make sense of John's obsession…

'You may not be,' Max bit out forcefully. 'But I certainly am.' He took both her hands in both of his, his gaze intense on the paleness of her face now. 'January, I intend giving Jude notice that I will no longer be available to work for him.'

She frowned. 'Because of those things I said to you?' she groaned self-reproachfully. 'But I didn't mean them. I was only—'

'No, not because of anything you said to me,' Max assured her firmly. 'I intended telling him all this anyway when I got back to America.'

She blinked. 'You did?'

He nodded. 'January, this is no excuse, I know, but since my mother walked out on my father and me when I was five, I've been pretty determined not to let anyone into my life—particularly a woman—who might hurt me like that again. But you—' He broke off, shak-